INTERCEPTION CITY

by

Parker T. Mattson

This is a work of total fiction. Names, places, characters and incidents are solely the product of the author's imagination and are used fictitiously, although references may be made to existing locations. Any resemblance to actual persons, living or dead, business establishments, events or even locales is entirely coincidental.

This one's dedicated to my sweetheart
of a wife, Ellen

"The truth may or may not set you free, but it can definitely get you killed."
Jim Starke

Also By Parker T. Mattson
Killing Liberty
Tropic Heat

Parker T. Mattson

Chapter 1

Interception City

Jim Starke didn't drink.

Not anymore. A rawboned Florida original of thirty-eight who spent his days in ragged shorts playing computer games, he did smoke, but was down to less than ten cigarettes a day, sometimes less than five. The generic brand, or lack of a brand, suited him fine.

He wasn't particular.

He lived alone in an overgrown trailer park stuck in a swampy corner of Interception City, the city itself stuck in an even swampier corner of Banyan County, all of it located so far off the main highway it barely appeared on even the most detailed maps of the deep southern Florida Everglades.

And then was often misspelled.

Interception City's longtime mayor, George Elliott, a decent-enough 78-year-old ex-bootlegger married to a slightly overweight but attractive 19-

year-old high school dropout from Peach Grove, Georgia, believed the map misspellings were somehow purposeful and, for whatever obscure reason, directed at him.

Each year he responded with a mean-spirited missive threatening to drive up to Atlanta, the site of the Palomar Map Company, and beat the living crap out of every single Palomar employee.

So far, his threats had been entirely ignored.

The Interception City locals, not much on spelling anyway, simply called the place I.C. or, less commonly, I.C. City, which, although wrong, somehow felt right to a certain percentage of them. They were a luckless lot of just under fifteen hundred hardcore rednecks and outright hicks, entirely unappreciated for the most part and so shit-poor destitute not a single legitimate double-wide could be found within the city limits.

Jim Starke didn't eat.

He'd lost his appetite years ago. He grew tomatoes, radishes, a few skinny watermelons and small bunches of thick, tough little bananas alongside and behind his trailer. Two boxes of generic bran flakes, a box of elbow macaroni, four cans of peas, a plastic jar of peanut butter and a large bag of nameless potato chips filled his narrow cupboards.

In his ancient Amana refrigerator, he kept mustard, two jars of pickles (sweet gherkins and baby dill), cocktail sauce, an untouched one-year-old six-pack of cheap Mexican beer and a cocked and locked compact H&K .45 semi-automatic pistol with an extended threaded barrel, the well-oiled gun stored under a half-dozen slowly blackening oranges in the right lower crisper drawer.

He disliked milk, ate his cereal dry by the handful, drank mostly unsweetened iced tea when he drank anything at all. Water didn't much interest him.

Jim Starke didn't work.

He didn't need to. There wasn't much to buy in Interception City. The weather-beaten trailer he owned (a *mobile home*, damn it, to the other residents) had been paid for long ago. It was worth far less than the generous Florida Homestead Exemption, so property taxes weren't an issue.

His Jeep, a barn-red-housepaint-over-rust CJ5 without carpeting, a top or even doors, was so old he could barely recall what year he'd bought it, much less what he'd paid for it. Car payments weren't a concern.

He had no interest in travel, or the rest of the country, or the rest of the world, for that matter. Thanks to the military, he'd seen more than enough of the world, and its trouble spots, and the horrors of anyplace outside the so-called civilized world, really, to last him well into old, older and even oldest age.

Interception City (Inter*section* City, according to last year's Palomar Map Company map) was more than world enough for him.

Jim Starke hadn't killed anybody.

Not lately. Every month the U.S. Government sent a green check to his P.O. box up in Clewiston. It was more than enough to cover his meager living expenses in the shitbox city he'd grown up in.

Where he now just sat out the world.

He sometimes felt he had no life, no liberty, and certainly not the right to the pursuit of happiness. On the other hand, his mind was just as often blank of any thoughts whatsoever (a mental trick he'd picked up in southeast Asia), the man living in the purest of present moments, that is.

And so any regrets he harbored barely had time to take hold.

It was not that he was merely invisible, though—much of the time it was as if Jim Starke didn't even exist.

Chapter 2

On a late Friday summer afternoon, a scorching ninety-six-degree pants-burner with no let-up in sight, Jim Starke sprawled naked and spent with Edna June Thurman in the near-darkness of his bedroom. She was his best friend's mother and the weirdness of their coupling had not escaped him.

It had, in fact, given him much pause over the years.

Directly beneath his trailer, in the relative cool of dirt-smelling shade and tropical undergrowth, Jim could hear one or more of the small green lizards skittering along the tin dwelling's corroded underside in a never-ending search for tasty and nutritious insects. Nearby, a large swamp bird raucously called out, its throaty vocal beacon answered almost immediately by its presumed mate.

Jim nodded to himself at the familiar sounds.

"My God," Edna June murmured, breathless. "You've killed me."

"I *did* give it everything there at the end," Jim admitted.

At fifty-four but looking fifteen years younger, Mrs. Edna June Thurman still got more than her share of hungry looks.

A statuesque green-eyed brunette of unsubtle beauty, she exuded a pure sexuality so potent it could almost be bottled and sold. Lying next to Jim, the radiant heat and perfumed odor of her firm body wildly evident, she wore only a lacy black garter belt and a pair of black nylons she'd ordered through a Victoria Secrets catalogue she openly considered 'smutty.'

She was currently the Vice Principal at I.C. High School and somewhat of a prude, at least officially.

Her clothes, a lightweight tan summer suit and white rayon blouse, were folded neatly at the far end of the couch in Jim's front room where they'd started. Her purse, shoes, beige nylons and sensible white bra and panties were next to them.

Thirty minutes earlier, she'd come into Jim's narrow hotbox of a trailer and immediately undressed without preamble, then slipped just as quickly into the black garter belt and black nylons.

A moment later, she was on her knees before him.

"The windows," Jim protested, without effect, trying to back away but not actually managing it. She never listened. "Damn it, Mrs. Thurman!"

She would always be *Mrs. Thurman* to him: he'd known Edna June his entire life, but he only really got to know her that Thanksgiving he was 14 and she was 30 and gave him his first blow job.

He'd certainly enjoyed that first time, of course.

And the youthful elements of both delicious surprise and secrecy in the Thurman's overheated kitchen pantry had particularly enchanted him, but there had been a long period of time when crushing guilt over their ongoing clandestine adventures, especially throughout his high school years, had troubled him greatly.

Gradually, however, the sound of his own conscience had eroded to a mere murmur of occasional protest when it came to Edna June.

Or to anything else, for that matter.

As Edna June had continued, rug-burned knees ignored, Jim watched the heat-warped trailer windows with one eye, her eager efforts with the other. His concerns at that moment were mostly regarding the neighbors rather than his and Edna June's near-lifetime of secret sexual activity.

The neighboring trailers were close and closer and, more importantly, the other residents (mostly elderly and without affluence) had scant little else to hold their attention. Edna June Thurman's monthly visits were certainly a matter of record and prolonged conversation by now, if only within the Paradise Acres Mobile Home Park, but Jim saw no reason to openly admit it.

Much less put on a public display.

Chapter 3

Four miles away, and kitty-corner from the one-story red-brick building that housed the combination I.C. City Hall and I.C. Police Department, the I.C. Convenience Store stood at the only intersection with a traffic light in the city.

Unpainted concrete block, two uncovered rust-pitted gas pumps and a fly-specked glass front covered with old flyers and posters, the I.C. Convenience Store was owned by Jim Starke's lifelong best friend, Horace Thurman, Jr., and Horace's father, Horace Thurman, Sr.

Horace Thurman, Sr. was, in fact, Edna June Thurman's elderly but devoted and lawfully wedded husband.

Behind the cash register at the I.C. Convenience Store that late Friday afternoon stood Thurman Jr. himself, 6'3" and corded with lean, wiry muscle, his chest as unyielding as a tree trunk. A thin straight-razor scar ran across his nose and cheek, the result of a dangerous and prolonged fight which he had (unsurprisingly) won.

He was not a man who anyone in town could ever recall losing.

While two other customers watched in shock, Thurman Jr. yanked a would-be redneck customer across the counter by the hair.

Thurman Jr. smashed the greasy man's face into the counter with a sickening thud. Then, still gripping the man's hair tightly, he reached across and retrieved a small canned ham from the redneck's large side jacket pocket.

He let the moaning redneck slide to the floor.

"Anybody know this sorry S.O.B.?"

One of the local customers, of indeterminate years in faded gray overalls, looked to him in surprise.

"Hell, no, Thurman," the man said. "No one in I.C.'d be shitfire crazy enough to steal from *you*. He's gotta be passing through—"

Thurman Jr. tossed the canned ham to the floor.

It landed with a flat thud directly in front of the moaning redneck's contorted face. The redneck managed to open one eye.

He slowly focused on the can with dawning horror.

"Kick his ass out of here," Thurman Jr. said. "And let him keep the ham, he needed it that bad."

The customer in gray overalls gave him another look of pure surprise.

"Why...you're a damn saint, Thurman."

Thurman Jr. simply gave the man back a look, then held it.

His gray eyes were neutral, like a reptile's, without a trace of humanity. The local man's smile froze; a scant moment later beads of sweat literally popped out on his broad forehead.

The skeletal face of Death itself couldn't have unnerved him more.

As far as most of the population of I.C. was concerned, Thurman Jr. was a certified lunatic, but without the bother of actual certification. In any case, lunatic or not, he was also correctly regarded as the most dangerous son of a bitch in all of Banyon County.

Thurman Jr. finally looked away from the local man, then wiped the redneck's blood off the counter with a shop rag he kept next to the sawed-off double-barrel Mossberg 12-gauge shotgun hidden below.

"Who's next?"

At the rear of the store, unseen by Thurman Jr. or any of the other locals, a second redneck, the older and wiser traveling companion of the bloody and nearly unconscious redneck being dragged out the front door, shakily sneaked a package of Kraft Colby Cheese out of his pocket and back into the cooler.

No way was he going to risk his life trying to get past a convenience store owner who was clearly a fucking psychopath.

Chapter 4

The unsettling notion that Thurman Jr. might one day learn about Jim Starke's physical relationship with his mother had kept Jim awake more than one troubled night over the years.

Without question, one of them would end up deader than hell.

It was a common enough story in I.C., or anywhere down south, really, for a local redneck to kill a best friend, usually during a drunken brawl involving firearms, broken bottles or knives.

Of course, it was one thing to kill a long-time buddy over dope, moonshine, a gambling debt, a woman or a beloved dog; it was another entirely to stumble across that same good friend sexing up your mom.

Even a Southern hanging judge might see the justice in that one.

Unfortunately though, as often as Jim had considered ending it with Thurman Jr.'s mother (serious issues of both personal safety and loyalty at stake, at least in the early years), it was damn near impossible to resist Mrs. Thurman's urgent sexual needs when she was in the mood.

She was just too damn good.

When she'd first arrived that afternoon, getting mostly naked and dropping to her knees in front of Jim, he knew she was just getting started.

"The bedroom," Jim had suggested. "The bed, the bed."

And, amazingly enough, she agreed, nodding almost imperceptibly, but unwilling to disengage, so that he had to *lead* her, as it were, toward the relative privacy of his bedroom.

They moved awkwardly, stiffly, with a scuttling, stopping and starting crablike motion, she moving on her knees, slowly, rug-burn ignored, unwilling to stop, across the entire front room.

In the process, both of them caught a quick but unmistakable glimpse of old Mr. Randolph from two trailers down, innocently passing by and looking positively startled at their openly indecent activity through the side window.

"Perfect," Jim said almost inaudibly, making unfortunate momentary eye contact with the elderly man, and in attempting to hurry along nearly choked Edna June.

"Ack!" she squawked.

To her, he managed, "Sorry."

And then they were in the bedroom, where, even as he succeeded in mostly closing the yellowing ancient blinds before falling onto the bed, she continued to put a genuine effort into pleasing him.

"I hope old Mr. Randolph's okay," Jim said. "He had an extremely weird look on his face."

She looked up.

"You mean when you just about choked me?"

"I said I was sorry."

"Yes, that makes it all better," she assured him, shaking her head.

Jim just gave her a look.

* * *

An hour and forty minutes later, Jim Starke walked naked out of the bedroom into the kitchen.

His was a lifetime tan, his sun-bleached-to-white blond hair cut military style, the two scars (a puckered through-and-through bullet hole at his shoulder, another on his lower back) from his earlier U.S. Army career evident.

He opened the Amana refrigerator.

The light didn't go on, the tiny bulb partially unscrewed. His eyes didn't bother going to the H&K handgun in the crisper; he knew it was always there, always cocked and locked.

Jim took a cigarette from a generic pack on the Amana's top shelf, closed the refrigerator door, then leaned down and lit it from the gas stove. The burner popped loudly when it ignited, but he didn't react, not even when the flame slightly singed his hair.

Edna June, hearing the burner, called out, "Jim, I thought you quit."

"I'm down to 4 and a half a day."

He looked up to see her appear in the bedroom doorway, a brunette Sharon Stone look-alike in the black nylons and garter belt.

She smiled at him, a little self-consciously, he thought.

"We're not finished yet," she said.

And so they weren't.

Chapter 5

Orlando

Almost two hundred miles northeast, in an exclusive community of huge pastel homes set on an emerald green golf course just outside Orlando, Wendy Jamison-Johnson stood resolutely in her fourteen-year-old daughter's Olympian-sized bedroom of pale peach and oyster.

"You're going," Wendy told the girl.

"Mother, I don't want to know your white trash family!"

"Pack. And they're your white trash family, too."

In jeans and a light silky blouse, with merely a touch of simple gold jewelry at her throat and wrist, Wendy was a particularly appealing woman in her late thirties, yet as likely to be in her early-twenties on a good night with the proper makeup and lighting. This astounded those trusted few friends who knew her real age.

Her secret, of course, was skin tone: through no doing of her own, Wendy possessed perfect skin, naturally smooth and unblemished still, for her age.

Or any age.

She was also slim and moderately tall at five seven, with fine delicate features and wide, expressive eyes so brightly blue the Sony Multi-Format HD TV cameras always honed in on them for close-ups as if magnetically attracted to their flawless color.

Her hair, though naturally blonde, was tinted, but only minimally so, and was full and thick, worn stylishly and boyishly short, upswept, and looked every bit as lustrous as it had twenty years earlier.

Unfortunately, these days, she did not feel as good as she looked.

"You are going," Wendy announced to her daughter, again, her patience at its end, her nerves finally on the verge of just snapping. "We're leaving very early in the morning."

"I don't *want* to go," the girl said yet again.

"I'm not going to argue."

She was not normally a pushy mother, but this was the decision she'd made and, although unnerving, she felt it was best for both herself and her daughter. In any case, Wendy *hoped* it was for the best.

The last three and a half weeks had been hellish for her, what with the sudden bankruptcy filing and the cancellation of her wildly successful cable television show, *'Psychic Trailer Park Hotline.'*

Worse was that the idiotic creditors had assigned *her* all the blame.

Any reasonable person willing to examine the facts, or just the books, could see her soon-to-be-ex-husband Leonard had been at the root of it all. The problem all along, of course, had been his scheming, lying ways, his sneaky treachery, so unseemly and (more importantly, for his sake) so *unlikely* for a federal judge.

It had been pathetically easy for him to arrange it so *she* became the villain, exactly as he had planned, while he appeared as only a shocked victim of his wife's duplicity when all the show's available cash, forty two thousand dollars and fifty three cents to be exact, mysteriously disappeared from the company checking account twenty-four hours before the twice-monthly payroll was due.

It also happened to be just three days after she'd surprised the man with a request for a divorce.

It was merely one more way for Federal Judge Leonard G. Johnson to demonstrate, as always, that he was in control of absolutely every facet of her life. And that he would remain so.

Of course, that wouldn't continue to be true if Wendy had anything to say about it. Which she absolutely did.

In addition, her on-air psychics (ha!) had abruptly turned on her, wanting their money immediately after the show's cancellation. Which was understandable, because the motley group of twenty-seven women and three men each lived on the constant brink of financial chaos. Their supposed psychic ability to help others apparently blinded them to the nature of their own monthly financial requirements and expenditures.

They were also unable to divine that it was Federal Judge Leonard Johnson who was the criminal here, not Wendy, for it was she alone who received the nearly non-stop stream of harassing phone calls, usually after midnight, demanding payment for their final two weeks of on-air enlightenment.

Reflecting on those last horrible three and a half weeks, Wendy wondered again if this was somehow life's payback, which she had long expected but which miraculously had not as yet arrived.

Admittedly, she felt an ongoing sense of guilt about past indiscretions, long-ago indiscretions of a sexual nature, actually, mostly back in high school as an idiot teen. These were issues she'd never fully faced.

Or resolved.

As far as her divorce was concerned, she'd been absolutely (if blindly and *stupidly*) faithful to her husband during their many years of marriage. But there was more than one difficult issue— again, of a past sexual nature—she knew she might one day find herself dealing with.

And upon occasional reflection, especially late at night, it gave her more than one cringing moment of deep regret.

It was also true, though, that her horrifying home life (with a family in I.C. she hadn't been able to even *think* about for the past twenty years) might have driven anyone slightly insane.

In any case, she needed to find a way out of her current predicament, and quickly, before she just lay down right there and let herself expire, permanently, out of sheer exhaustion.

She was so tired of fighting.

"Mother, you haven't seen them in twenty years," Jennifer, an expert on *everything* at 14, announced. "Your terrible family."

She was the mirror image of Wendy, every bit as beautiful and almost as tall, although slimmer and even more finely blonde. Her blue eyes were blazing with anger and resentment.

"Now you want *me* to know them?"

Wendy took a deep breath to steady herself.

"I want you to just *meet* them," she tried again. "Then, of course, you can decide for yourself. . ."

Jennifer studied her mother as if seeing her for the first time.

She had the ability, like her snake of a father (who the girl adored, to hell with the truth about the evil lying son of a bitch), the unnerving ability, in fact, to make a person feel suddenly dissected, pinned down and spread open almost, so that the object of this scrutiny knew they were being seen in the most unflattering light imaginable.

It was a trick of facial expression, or merely attitude perhaps, that both father and daughter had somehow mastered, Wendy believed, to make other people, *all* other people, feel inferior.

That it still worked, even on her, knowing it was merely a trick of sorts, irritated Wendy no end.

"You and Daddy both hate your loser family," the girl said. "And he's never even met them!"

"What your father thinks no longer concerns me."

"*You* said you'd never set foot again in Interception City."

"You're going. We'll be back by Sunday afternoon."

"We'll probably be murdered or something!"

"You're going," Wendy said, for the last time. "It won't kill you."

"They'll be drunk all the time!"

"Start packing."

"They'll be having sex with farm animals!"

"Don't be ridiculous." In truth, Wendy was not about to argue *that* one. "And, it's not a farm."

"I'm going to throw up."

"It'll only be for a little while."

"Just tell me *why*? Why do I have to go?"

Her mother had no intention of going into the details. Not yet.

She pointed to the large beige designer suitcase with brass fittings which she'd gotten out of her own closet for Jennifer. She'd left it open on the girl's expansive bed. As yet, not a single item had been placed within.

"Pack."

Chapter 6

The late afternoon fun was just beginning in a not-so-nice part of Orlando off of Orange Blossom Trail at the Viceroy Motel. It was a well-known haven of crack whores, crack dealers and general crack-heads.

Other illegal drugs of choice were available for the right price, but the Viceroy's specialty was crack, pure and simple.

The mostly-absentee owner felt it paid to specialize.

It was a one-story, L-shaped structure of aged white brick, each room opening directly into a heat-soaked and pot-holed parking lot that contained a motley assortment of battered older cars, a couple of rusty bicycles and several scruffy, lurking-about characters.

Inside Room 104, with the door and heavy smoke-smelling drapes closed, a particularly scruffy young black crack addict was lurking about, strung out, pacing rapidly, trying to think clearly.

"I just need to know it's safe," he said with agitation.

He was addressing two tough-looking men, one white, one Spanish, each sitting at the end of the two narrow twin beds. They both wore sports coats, dress slacks and open-necked shirts.

"But I'm getting a nervous vibe here."

The tough-looking Spanish man, the taller of the two, suddenly stood, acted like he didn't understand.

"What the fuck are you saying?" he demanded.

Next door, in Room 102, two experienced undercover officers from the Florida Department of Law Enforcement (FDLE), Kevin Jenkins and Murphy Parcel, watched and listened to a video monitor wirelessly linked to a micro-camera disguised inside a broken light-fixture high on the urine-stained wall in Room 104.

(That anyone could pee that high had caused a sense of genuine wonderment in both Jenkins and Parcel when they'd earlier installed the state-of-the-art surveillance system: "What, was this guy standing on a fucking ladder?!").

"Now what?" Jenkins asked his partner, on the monitor seeing the possibility of their entire operation falling apart. "What the hell...?"

In Room 104, the tough white man stood also, scowling at the jumpy young black addict. This wasn't the way it was supposed to go down.

"You're fucked up," he said.

The black addict gave him a look.

"I got allergies…"

"Sure."

Unseen by either the video surveillance camera or the two tough-looking men, there were two cheap .38 handguns stuck into the back of the young black addict's pants, both gun handles wrapped in dark masking tape.

His nose was running, his eyes bloodshot. Without looking away or turning his back, he wiped his nose with the closer bedspread.

The two tough-looking men were clearly disgusted.

"Word is out," the young black man said, "that you two fuckers are cops…so I'm hesitating to complete our transaction."

The tough Spanish man shook his head.

"You're not making friends here calling 'cop.'"

"Finish the transaction or go fuck yourself," the tough white man added. "And maybe you're the cop."

The young addict was stunned at the accusation.

"That's exactly what a cop'd say!"

He was getting more agitated, more paranoid, started rubbing his face as if spiders were crawling over it.

While the two men silently watched, he said:

"I'm sweating to death here!" He looked to them, then decided. "I'm not doing this, not today.

Let me see you two gentlemen to the door—we'll do this tomorrow."

The tough-looking white man and tough-looking Spanish man exchanged a quick glance, decided for themselves as well.

"There's not going to be a tomorrow," the white man said.

And he and the Spanish man both moved apart as they reached under their sports coats for their weapons. The young black addict, realizing, suddenly pulled both guns from behind his back with blinding speed and without hesitation shot them both many times.

The quick explosive sounds were almost deafening.

The tough white man barely got his gun out, got one wild shot off before getting knocked down. The tough Spanish man, shot dead-center through the chest three times, landed on his back on the tiled floor with one leg sticking straight up beside the farther bed.

Both dead before anyone could take a quick breath.

In Room 102 next door, both undercover cops jumped to their feet with yelps of surprise, yanked out their own guns.

"Son of a bitch...!" Jenkins said.

A scant moment later, the door to Room 104 crashed open inwardly, the cheap door frame splintering, and both Jenkins and Parcel rushed in.

The young black crack addict stood over the two dead men, both guns still out and smoking like an old Western. Blood was everywhere.

"Jesus Christ...!" Parcel said.

The young black addict looked to him.

"I know," was all he said.

"The Lieutenant's going to be super-pissed, Walter," Jenkins said, putting away his gun as Parcel checked the two dead drug dealers for signs of life. "What the hell were you thinking?"

Walter Hightower, at twenty-three the youngest undercover officer with the Florida Department of Law Enforcement and the recent *crack addict* (a part he'd perfected over the past month), said simply:

"It was me or them."

Jenkins gave the young officer a long look.

"When the Lieutenant gets on your ass over this," he said, ruefully, "you're gonna wish it was you."

Walter looked to him, then back to the two men he'd killed. There was definitely going to be trouble.

It wasn't his first fatal shootout on the job, however much justified, and he knew it would only add to his not-entirely-kidding reputation in the department as a serious badass.

Maybe even a born killer.

"Fuck."

Chapter 7

Interception City

"I suppose you heard that Wendy Jamison, that fake TV psychic *slut,* is coming back for the I.C. High School Reunion tomorrow night after all these years."

Edna June had said it as she started gathering up her clothes.

Jim had not heard even a hint of such a thing.

"Where'd you hear that?"

"What a joke..." she continued, with a disgusted shake of her head. "All those morons spending money for that ignorant psychic nonsense! Then she goes bankrupt! Why didn't she see *that* coming?"

"Wendy wasn't supposed to be one of the psychic's," Jim pointed out. "She was just the producer and the host."

Edna June gave him a look.

"She was just the biggest whore in the history of I.C. High. She screwed *everybody*, but you couldn't make a move on her."

He remembered well enough.

Jim hadn't seen or talked to Wendy since their high school days, over twenty years earlier. Not in person, at least.

He had, of course, watched her cable television call-in show occasionally, marveling at how skinny and gorgeous she'd managed to remain (as she approached so-called middle age) as she stood in front of her phone banks of 'psychics' at 2:00 A.M., telling those late-night viewers at home:

"Ladies, my Trailer Park Psychics know exactly what that lying son of a bitch of yours is doing right this second! That's right, I said 'son of a bitch'!"

And the phones would start ringing off the hook.

The girl/woman he used to know definitely had stage presence. Meaning, charisma and confidence, a lot of it.

He also remembered Wendy Jamison abruptly leaving for Orlando the moment she'd graduated. That sudden move on Wendy's part had surprised no one more than Jim Starke, who, although aware of Wendy Jamison's wild nature and one of her closest friends, had nonetheless been extremely...*smitten* with her throughout high school.

Not that he'd done anything about it. Or said anything to her about it.

Of course, back then there also was her reputation (bad, bad, bad) to consider, which seemed to matter so much in those days.

In any case, it had nearly killed him when she dropped so completely out of his world, and everyone's world, without a word to him or anyone else, and headed up to the big city, never to return.

And then, years later, out of nowhere, she suddenly appeared on her late-night cable show in Orlando, hosting it, the '*Psychic Trailer Park Hotline*,' catering to the ultimate niche market: trailer park denizens needing immediate psychic guidance to resolve the bizarre predicaments of their lives.

That is, as long as they provided the necessary credit card information.

* * *

Edna June stepped into her rayon skirt, yanked it up over her firm hips, hooked it quickly, and reached for her white blouse.

"She was screwing everybody," she said again, "and you couldn't make a move on her. And all the while I'm letting you do *anything* you wanted, and all you ever talked about was her. . ."

Jim gave Edna June a look.

"I was fifteen or sixteen. She was *my* age, okay? You were more like my mom—but blowing me."

"Don't get smart."

Her look said she wasn't kidding. He watched Mrs. Thurman button her blouse. She shook her head.

"They called her 'Wendy Bang' and 'Hot Box' and even 'Peanut Butter,' because she spread so easy, and that was just the teachers."

She was finished dressing. She looked to him. There was *something* odd going on with Edna June, something apparently upsetting, that was certain, but Jim really had no idea what.

When he didn't respond, the woman just shook her head.

"I'm late," she said, glancing at her silver watch. It was a birthday gift from her son Thurman, Jr. and Jim Starke more than twenty years earlier and she was never without it. "It's almost dark."

"Take the Old Grove Road shortcut," he suggested.

"You always say that," she said, not happily. "I'm out of gas and it's through the middle of nowhere."

"You could make it that far on fumes."

And Edna June Thurman suddenly brushed past him and left without another word, seemingly on the verge of tears.

Jim, watching her go, had no idea why.

Chapter 8

Police Chief Orville Goody of Interception City was as murderous a man as ever lived—except, perhaps, for his skinny, slack-jawed and mouth-breathing son-in-law Ray Lanyard, who was not only genuinely murderous, but twice as mean.

Ray at thirty-four was married to Police Chief Goody's seventeen-year-old daughter, Virginia, and he was the police chief's right-hand-man, Officer Ray Lanyard, a position he used to his every unfair advantage.

"Goddamnit, Ray!" the police chief berated him.

As usual.

Orville Goody was a large man, well over six feet tall and fat, going to pork, really, and he was already sweating, streaks of his greasy brown hair, thinning badly and combed across on top, plastered down on his forehead.

"Have you got wet manure in that stupid head of yours?" he continued. "Lift your end when I lift mine!"

"Sorry, Chief," the other man murmured, not looking up, and lifting.

It was dusk, their white and black Chevrolet I.C. police cruiser down a seldom used red-dirt grove road, parked along a curve and at an angle to a stand of slash pine and laurel oak that partially obstructed the view of the car, the two men and the deep canal behind them.

Out of the open trunk, they were hauling a tightly bound, very dead young black man named Elmore Hightower. He'd been carefully, and heavily, weighted down with rusted angle iron.

Ray Lanyard had earlier shot the man four times at close range.

Most of the wiser folks in Interception City considered Officer Ray to be an absolute weasel, and dumber than a rotten stump (Chief Goody himself was thought to be the embodiment of heartless evil itself), but few were naive enough to voice such thoughts out loud.

It was pretty well understood that occasionally a troublesome prisoner 'escaped,' only to be eventually found at the bottom of a swampy pit or hidden lake, 'gator-gnawed and entangled in baling wire and cement blocks or angle iron. Positive identification, of course, was then often difficult and these escape-and/or-murder cases remained on the books for years, marked *Open* as if someone within the I.C. police department was actively pursuing hot leads.

In reality, no one believed such a farfetched idea for a second, but these intermittent gruesome discoveries kept most folks pretty much in line in Interception City and even across Banyon County.

Meaning:

No one with any percentage of a working brain desired to run afoul of either Police Chief Orville Goody or Officer Ray Lanyard.

It wasn't healthy.

As for the dead black man, he was neither an escaped prisoner nor even a resident of I.C. or Banyon County. Rather, from Orlando many miles north, Elmore Hightower was misfortunate enough to have connected with Virginia Lanyard via the Internet, where Ray's long hours of casual bullying, petty graft and enforcing the law with his father-in-law gave his young bride plenty of opportunities to sit at her computer keyboard exploring the more urgent and unusual aspects of her sexuality with wildly curious strangers.

"This is a real heavy motherfucker," Ray complained, struggling to lift the man out by the shoulders. "He looks skinny."

"Lift him out, set him down and shut up. Maybe if you hadn't put so much lead in him, he wouldn't weigh so much. Or if you were man enough to control your wife, we wouldn't be out here in the first damn place. . ."

Ray saw no advantage in mentioning that all four bullets, steel-jacketed, had passed clean through without much slowing down, so no longer constituted any of the man's actual dead weight. The last comment also, concerning his young wife, Ray carefully chose to ignore; it was the continuation of an on-going argument he could never hope to win.

The Police Chief held no illusions about his sweet little daughter's morals.

But he *had* hoped her marriage to Ray Lanyard just over a year ago at sixteen might settle down the girl, might help stabilize her uninhibited nature through the influence of an older, supposedly more mature man.

This had not happened.

If anything, Ray—far weaker in spirit and intellect than the slim teen—had allowed himself to be molded by the girl to meet her every need, expectation and whim, instead of the other (far more normal, as far as Police Chief Orville Goody was concerned) way around.

Within two months, this surrender of his masculine duty by Ray to his young bride was so immediately obvious to the police chief that he instantly lost what little respect he had had for his long-time friend.

"Her marriage to you has been a disaster," the Chief added, genuinely distraught. "She coulda picked a better man out of a lineup. Now she's meeting black men on the Internet for sex..."

"She didn't get to meet this one—"

The Police Chief merely gave him a look.

"Hold his head steady. . ."

Elmore Hightower had been handsome in life, and at twenty-seven had been as concerned about his appearance as most good-looking young men are, but in death his expression was forever frozen into an open-mouthed grimace of surprise.

A single gold tooth shone brightly in front.

"I want that tooth," Police Chief Goody said.

With the butt of his chrome-plated Dan Wesson .357 Magnum revolver, he hunkered down with noticeable exertion and tapped at the gold tooth while Ray held the back of the man's head steady against the ground.

"You idiot," the police chief told him. "Tilt it slightly. I don't want to search down a damn dead man's throat if he swallows it."

Ray tilted the head, Police Chief Goody tapped harder, and the tooth broke free, then fell into the corner of the man's mouth. The police chief picked it out, studied it, then put it into his pocket.

He stood with a gasp of effort.

Both men looked up at the sound of a large vehicle, approaching fast.

A black Toyota FJ Cruiser was making its way quickly down Old Grove Road, seen sporadically through the trees. It followed the ruts unevenly as it bounced along. Before the police chief or Officer Ray could react, it passed into the open as it followed the curve, then pulled alongside the I.C. police cruiser.

It crunched to a sudden stop at the sight of them.

"Is there a problem?" the woman at the wheel called out as soon as the darkly tinted window slid down. "Anything I can do...?"

And the Police Chief immediately recognized Edna June Thurman, the Vice Principal at I.C. High.

She was, in fact, one of the few nervy minority who had worked so hard (and futilely) against his continued employment in years past, repeatedly labeling his department not only corrupt and vile but genuinely evil. He knew she truly detested him.

Of course, the feeling was decidedly mutual.

Edna June glanced at the I.C. police cruiser's open trunk, then down at the dead young black man on the ground. Baling wire and strips of rusted angle iron did not seem a natural accouterment to the khaki slacks and bloody button-down dress shirt worn by the body.

That they were strapped to him as the result of an oddball one-in-a-million accident seemed highly unlikely.

She stiffened, and then, jamming it back into first gear, immediately floored the accelerator and popped the clutch to rocket away. Instead, with too much clutch, too fast, the big vehicle abruptly stalled.

The big Toyota SUV sat in embarrassed silence for only a scant moment, then started again.

Police Chief Goody swung his chrome .357 Magnum up into Edna June's face and with a fat thumb pulled back the hammer. It made an oily, substantial click filled with the weight of absolute and deadly authority.

He gave her a long sobering moment to stare down the heavy barrel.

"Don't," was all he said.

Edna June slid her hand over to her cell phone in the console, covertly pressed the programmed 8-button for Jim Starke's cell phone. It softly beeped through the seven-digit number it was calling.

Police Chief Goody, stepping up onto the running board, pushed his considerable bulk far enough through the open window into the vehicle and across her to reach the keys. His eyes lit on the cell phone, glanced to her, then motioned for her to hand it to him.

Edna June shrank back, stiffly, clearly too afraid to even breathe, much less let out the clutch again. She mutely handed him the cell phone. He turned it off, handed it to Officer Ray behind him, then reached in again and turned off the ignition as well.

He quickly discovered he couldn't find the catch to pull the keys out. He swore to himself, left the damn keys dangling.

Finally, he stepped back onto the ground and turned his attention once again to Edna June, pointing the large gun directly between her eyes.

"Sorry, Miz Thurman, but you're gonna have to step down out of that vehicle."

And he smiled slowly, showing flat horse-like teeth when he said it.

Chapter 9

It was already dark out.

Jim Starke sat at his laptop computer playing a somewhat addictive first-person shooter game called *Kill or Be Killed*, the narrow living room lit only by a combination of the screen, the tiny range hood light over the kitchen stove and the faint glow of his third cigarette of the day.

He took a deep drag, then let it out slowly.

He was trying to quit, it was true, but he often (at least lately) found himself wondering if he really had all that much to actually live for. Of course, the fact that Wendy Jamison was suddenly returning to I.C. for the high school reunion had just that very afternoon altered his thinking.

Anything was suddenly possible again.

He put the cigarette out in a cheap tin ashtray he'd lifted from exactly the kind of motel it belonged in, then picked up the open can of cold peas he was eating from with a spoon. He had early in his life decided eating canned peas with a fork was simply too much trouble.

A moment earlier, his cell phone had rang briefly with a muffled sound. Jim opened the drawer of his computer desk, took out the cell phone, saw that Edna June Thurman had called but then immediately hung up.

Or been disconnected.

He re-dialed but got her voice mail instead. He tried it one more time, got the same voice mail.

Without leaving a message, he put back the phone, closed the drawer, and resumed playing *Kill or Be Killed.*

If she wanted to talk that badly, about *whatever* had been bothering her earlier that afternoon, he was certain she'd call back the next time she had a free moment. She always did.

Chapter 10

Orlando

Downtown was alive at night, as always, tourists and local Floridians alike moving slowly on I-4 and the East-West Expressway at the end of the day, miles of headlights going in all four directions.

Most were either heading home or travelling to and/or from the various major theme parks: Disney World, Universal Studios-Orlando, Sea World, as well as the other, much smaller specialty attractions such as Gatorland or Pioneer Village.

In an office behind an unmarked door in the 20-story Citrus Tower Building on Orange Avenue, the Florida Department of Law Enforcement's undercover post was surprisingly small. It was comprised mainly of four cluttered desks, several older office machines against the off-white walls and an huge array of paperwork taped and tacked onto several large bulletin boards.

Walter Hightower sat quietly at a desk along the far wall and slowly typed his report into one of the shared computers.

In sharp contrast to his earlier crack addict persona, he was an extremely handsome young man who wore a subtly-striped dark sports coat that barely concealed the walnut stock of the .44 Magnum he carried in a shoulder holster.

Lt. Dean Scribner, short, muscular and almost as wide as he was tall, stalked up to him, threw a case folder onto his desk.

"Hightower, your brother never got to the Conch Motel down in Key West. He hasn't called in and he won't answer his goddamn cell phone, which is getting everybody down there real fucking nervous!"

He was ready to explode with obvious frustration.

"The whole operation's in jeopardy," he added.

Walter looked to the case folder, then up to Scriber's glare.

"You know Elmore, Lieutenant. He always shows up...eventually."

"He's got that goddamn impound car, too."

The only other FDLE officer at her desk that night was Sgt. Graziana Rodriguez. She gave Walter an almost imperceptible glance of sympathy, but wisely kept her head down, concentrating on her paperwork.

Walter said, "My brother'll get there. My mother raised us right. He's not totally crazy. Not yet."

The Lieutenant didn't exactly agree.

"Yeah, not yet. But since his divorce, he's someone I don't even know. He's risking his career, his life and the entire undercover team when he pulls a disappearing stunt like this."

He studied Walter closely.

"Do you know where he is?"

Walter avoided answering, turned to him and gave Lieutenant Scriber a big, sincere smile. "If he doesn't call in soon," he said, patting his .44 Magnum, "I'll track the boy down and shoot the motherfucker my own damn self."

The Lieutenant was not amused.

"You only think you're kidding, Hightower, but that's exactly what you're doing. Hit the road. Now. And when you get back we're gonna have a talk about those two drug dealers you killed today."

Walter gave him a look.

"Like you said: *drug dealers*. It was me or them."

"Get moving."

Lt. Scribner turned and stalked back out of the room.

Sgt. Graziana Rodriguez finally looked up from her desk, shook her head at Walter with a cynical smile. She was a compact woman of forty, a FDLE officer almost her entire adult life. On the yearly shooting range qualification tests, she was as accurate and almost as quick on the draw as Walter himself.

He both respected and trusted her.

"So, Walter, where's Elmore tonight?"

Walter Hightower stood.

He exhaled slowly, seriously pissed off at his older brother.

He'd tried reaching Elmore on his cell phone earlier, many times, but to no avail. Now he'd have to get in his unmarked car in the damn middle of the night and drive for hours down to the middle of fucking nowhere, somewhere in the middle of the goddamn Florida Everglades, his least favorite place in the whole wide world.

Anyone with even minimal intelligence knew it was nothing but man-eating alligators, poisonous snakes and giant fucking mosquitos that could carry off a goddamn horse.

Fuck!

"Elmore's in a little swamp-town shithole he was stopping at on the way down to Key West," he told Graziana. "Chasing some hot-assed white trash pussy he met on the Internet."

At her sudden look, openly disapproving, Walter held up his hands and added:

"His words."

Chapter 11

Wendy looked through her large textured forest green suitcase one last time, then closed and latched the cover.

She'd picked jeans and shorts and simple tops and even simpler shoes, tennis shoes mainly, for the return to her hometown. In addition, she'd packed, carefully, a very simple yet elegant little black dress, with accessories and shoes to match, although she still wasn't certain she would actually wear it to the I.C. High School reunion.

Or even if she would attend.

She picked up the large suitcase and stepped out into the hall. It was heavy, and she was slim, but she was not weak.

The entire house was quiet and dark, except for her own room and (bright light visible under the door, muffled TV voices dramatically arguing) her teen daughter's bedroom.

"Get some sleep," she called out to Jennifer as she passed her door. "We're leaving *very* early in the morning, well before dawn. I don't want to deal with any weekend traffic..."

In answer, the medium-loud television within her daughter's bedroom was suddenly turned up louder.

"Great."

Wendy moved easily into the kitchen, putting her suitcase down in front of the door leading into the four-car garage. She opened the door, leaned out into darkness and pressed the garage door opener.

The overhead light came on as the nearer of the two double-doors creaked upward, brightness spilling out onto the darkened driveway as it allowed her access to the trunk of her gray Lincoln. The other large double space, now empty, with its own separate double garage door still closed, had been for Leonard's matching black Lincoln.

No longer being parked at the house.

Not after Wendy had made an unexpected visit to Leonard's private office in downtown Orlando at lunchtime four weeks earlier.

It was there she'd discovered bleached-blonde Cassandra Cassidy, his longtime assistant, naked from the waist up in his lap behind his large desk, the good-looking forty-something woman in a long flowing summer dress that had been pushed down around her hips.

Wendy's husband was fully dressed but his hands were both on her bare breasts, right where any damn person bursting into his private office with their own key might see.

Cassandra stood up surprisingly fast seeing Wendy, awkwardly pulling the top of her dress back up, thus blocking any immediate view Wendy might have of her cheating bastard son of a bitch husband.

Cassandra's long dress covered her legs discreetly to the floor, but her bright pink thong panties prominently featured on Leonard's dark green desk blotter attested to her nakedness underneath.

"Wendy!" the horrified clerical exclaimed. "Oh God, Wendy, I'm so sorry! So damn sorry!"

Leonard, instantly panicking but apparently thinking fast, said from behind the woman, "Wendy, she had a dress malfunction and I was helping out!" To his assistant, he managed, "Cassandra, that should be fine now..."

He wasn't too good under pressure, Wendy had long ago learned.

Not certain exactly how to react, and having had no clue her husband was boinking his hired help, she silently waved Cassandra aside.

And Cassandra, clearly feeling awful if not outright suicidal over this overt treachery to a younger woman long considered a friend, finally burst into fat tears, snatched up her panties and ran from the office.

Of course, not even remotely stupid, Wendy had long had her suspicions concerning Leonard, but not about Cassandra.

It irked her greatly, also, that she'd succeeded in remaining entirely faithful to the apparently worthless man throughout their many years of marriage.

"Wendy," he said at last, blinking.

But she was already gone.

Chapter 12

Wendy picked up her suitcase and carried it to the back of her Lincoln, setting it down while she fished the keys out of her pocket. Then she opened the trunk, richly carpeted and almost large enough to store a baby grand piano, should the need ever arise.

She jumped when a sweaty hand closed on her shoulder from behind.

"Jesus Christ!" her soon-to-be-ex-husband said, as startled as she. "Calm down, it's just me, the former love of your life."

Wendy brushed his hand off, then turned to him.

"Leonard, drop dead!"

She met his look without the slightest hint of affection or humor.

"How long have you been waiting out there?" she wanted to know. "Lurking about in the dark? You're not even supposed to be here."

In fact, her ex-husband was not supposed to be within one mile of their ex-home, without a prior appointment, approved by her, according to the domestic restraining order she'd managed to obtain.

Such an order was fairly rare against an actual sitting judge, and especially a Federal one, but, thank God, Wendy herself had made a few friends in high places over the years and she was, after all, in the right.

That, coupled with the fact that the man tried to strangle her when she told him they were finished, Leonard going completely berserk, in fact. And her story, true enough, apparently had the *ring* of truth to it as well, for her husband was immediately, after that, legally restrained.

She had not seen his face since.

"Leonard, I'll just say it once: get out."

He didn't seem overly concerned with her command, merely stood casually with his arms crossed in that condescending way of his and shook his head with genuine disappointment.

After all, he was in the garage of his own spacious and comfortable home.

He was five years older than she, a medium-sized five ten, with well-groomed sandy-colored hair and a straightforward, moderately handsome face, if just a fraction narrow. His easy smile was as openly friendly as it was false, cultivated over the years merely as a negotiating tool in the courtroom, long before he became an actual judge and no longer really required it.

It was now habit, pure and simple, and meant nothing to him or anyone else who knew him particularly well.

"I just want to talk," he said in his perfectly modulated tones, a man who never had to raise his voice. He was accustomed to the authority that came with the bench and it showed. "That's all, just talk. . ."

Wendy noticed that, while speaking, Leonard moved nonchalantly between the door leading back into the house and herself, subtly blocking her one true path of escape. Running in the other direction down the driveway and into the street in the middle of the night, making a big to-do and causing a scene for the neighbors, was not Wendy's style and her husband knew it.

"Are you carrying a gun?" she wanted to know.

For he normally did, concealed somewhere upon his expensively clad person. Tonight, he was wearing well-pressed white chino slacks, a light blue Brooks Brothers' oxford button-down shirt and a lightweight argyle sweater vest, even though it was hot as hell outside.

"Your little .32 automatic maybe, under your sweater?"

Her husband gave her an annoyed look.

"And why shouldn't a Federal judge carry a concealed weapon?" he asked. "One never knows..." And here he exhaled slowly. "Anyway, not tonight. No reason, is there, when we're just calmly talking?"

"We're not talking," Wendy pointed out. "You're breaking the law you're sworn to uphold, both as a lawyer and a judge, and I'm going back into the house as soon as you get out of my way."

And she finished putting her suitcase into the trunk of the big gray Lincoln and closed the lid. She then walked purposely back toward the door, straight through the very polite would-be strangler, if necessary, and was pleased when he actually took a step back out of the way.

"This is crazy," he said. "I am your husband and you are my wife. I made a stupid mistake with a woman who worked for me and I apologize, end of story, case closed. I let her go the very next day, which you'd already know *if* you'd let me speak to you before this very moment."

It was Wendy's turn to study the man she'd apparently been married to for far too many years.

"You strangled me, Leonard, or tried to," she pointed out. "Until I kneed you in the testicles. And you fired poor Cassandra because of something *you* made her do. I know you too well."

"I should've *never* given you that key—"

"I'm certain keeping her job had something to do with it. Doesn't she have two kids in junior high school and no husband?"

Leonard shrugged.

"I couldn't work with her any longer if you and I were to remain happily married, now could I?"

Wendy had to laugh.

"Leonard, we're not happily married," she told him. "Nor will we ever be again. I'm getting on with my life, bankrupt television show or not, and wait till I get a chance to tell my side of the story on *that!*"

From Leonard's expression, it was obvious the conversation was not going as he'd hoped.

"Wendy, you cannot divorce me because I will not let you," he said seriously. "I promise, if you persist in this, I will kill you dead, and I mean that with all my heart." He looked to her with genuine sadness. "I love you, you silly bitch, and you refuse to believe me..."

Well, there, it was finally said, she thought: the treat of death.

But Wendy Jamison was not a woman who rattled easily, even though she realized men actually *did* sometimes murder the women they loved. Seriously.

"Leonard, you embezzled over $40,000 from the show's account to keep me dependent on you, but you're not getting away with it. I'm meeting with the State Attorney in Tallahassee on Monday and I'm taking the books. You're going to be prosecuted."

It was as if she'd thrown a bucket of ice water in his face.

"You can't be serious!"

"Time to go, Leonard," she informed him.

And with that, she calmly walked over to the rack along the wall holding a variety of long-handled garden implements and took down a sharp five-foot-long metal weed digger.

She turned back and pointed it directly at him.

"If you *are* armed, Leonard, you better shoot me," she informed him. "Otherwise, unless you walk out of here right now, I'm going to hurt you so badly with this thing you'll wish you had."

And, with real purpose, she started toward him.

"They suspended me today," he told her suddenly, which stopped her. "They asked me to take a voluntary leave of absence until the restraining order issues are resolved. It's apparently not good form to have me working with a possible felony conviction hanging over my head, the strangling thing."

"Go, Leonard, right this second, and I won't report this."

"And, of course, everyone's a bit miffed that I had to let Cassandra go," he went on. "She was the most competent assistant the office had ever seen. Plus," and here he gave Wendy a rueful little smile, "I guess I wasn't the only one she was, uh, involved with..."

"I'm sorry it's such a mess," she told him, "I really am, but you must *leave*. You're starting to ramble, which is making me a little bit nervous. . ."

Chapter 13

In her huge 4-car garage, and facing her estranged and possibly dangerous husband, suspended Federal Judge Leonard Johnson, Wendy refused to take even a single step back.

The well-dressed man before her kept his eyes keenly focused on the sharp weed digger she held, but made no move in any direction. He didn't say anything for a very long moment, either, as if suddenly remembering something of utmost importance, but then, slowly, whatever it was seemed to just as suddenly slip away from him.

He looked to Wendy as if *she* might know what he'd been about to tell her, but she had even less of a clue.

She just wanted the man out of her garage.

Then the door leading to the house opened and their daughter Jennifer, barefoot in blue shorty pajamas, was standing in the doorway with a look of utter annoyance on her young face. She'd come down to the kitchen for a snack and was wondering who the hell was talking so loud out in the garage this time of night.

"Daddy!" she said, and was so happy to see him she walked out onto the cement floor and up to him without her slippers. "I thought you weren't supposed to be here. That's what Mom said."

And her eyes suddenly focused on the weed digger.

"What's going on?"

"Jennifer, your father's just leaving."

"I came by to see how you girls were doing," the man told her.

"Mom's taking me to Interception City," the girl suddenly complained. "For her stupid high school reunion tomorrow night."

Leonard looked positively startled at this sudden news, so clearly unexpected was it to him.

"So..." he said to Wendy. "You're going back to that open sewer where you were born—"

"Leonard, that's no longer any of your business."

"—the damaged wife, returning to the arms of a former greasy idiot boyfriend, no doubt."

"What?!" Jennifer suddenly blurted, disbelief filling her young face. "There's some old boyfriend? My God!"

And then she sniffled as a single tear formed in her eye and, a moment later, she started crying for real, bawling her blue eyes out at the sheer horror of it all, in fact, her future sad life unwinding before her like a swamp-lined, dimly-lit country road leading to nowhere.

What the *hell* was her mother thinking?!

"Jennifer, there *is* no boyfriend," Wendy told her daughter. And then, "Leonard, damn you!"

The slim blonde teen was shaking wildly now, convulsing almost, her entire body wracked with spasms as she gulped for air between sobs, trying to breathe, trying to calm herself, trying just to live.

Her perfect family, her perfect *life*, was being torn apart by her crazy-assed mom, for reasons she couldn't begin to comprehend.

"Oh, God..." she blubbered. "This can't be happening..."

"Leonard, you son of a bitch."

"Be brave, Jennifer," Leonard told their daughter. "We'll get through even this."

"Daddy, my God..." Jennifer continued her blubbering disapproval. "I think I'm going to throw up."

"*I'm* going to throw up," Wendy said.

And her grip tightened on the handle of the weed digger, causing the judge's eyes to widen almost imperceptibly. She took a step forward, towards him, but then the impulse raging through her to kill him, or at the least *hurt* him where he stood, quickly expended itself.

She tossed the tall garden implement to the floor.

"You're not worth it, Leonard," she told him. "I'll just let the State Attorney deal with you."

And with that she turned and walked back into the house.

Chapter 14

Interception City

At twenty minutes after midnight, Jim Starke pulled into the parking lot of *The Alligator Pit*.

The place was much less than a simple redneck bar in a tropical swamp; it was rather a redneck *hovel* in a tropical swamp, a dimly lit corrugated metal shed of three walls and a junky open porch area in back that faced into a tangle of dark impenetrable jungle.

Drinking at dusk in the place always meant mosquito bites, and a possible loose snake or two, but no patron, male or female, ever really seemed to notice or complain. A single weak streetlight in front provided the sole illumination for a large poorly hand-painted sign tacked next to the door that proclaimed 'Enter at Your Own Risk,' and 'No Negroes Please.'

The owner, 'Big Jeff' Welsher, thought this was hilarious.

There were several older cars and pickup trucks in the loose gravel patch that served as the parking lot, and alongside that, on the fringe area of the sparse brownish grass, rested a permanent collection of upright and tipped-over washing machines, electric ranges and refrigerators, all damaged beyond repair.

Jim Starke's battered CJ-5 Jeep fit right in.

He parked between a badly rusted S-10 pickup with a Confederate flag decal filling the entire rear window and a faded red 1976 Cadillac Eldorado with a gray primer door and a peeled-back vinyl roof of indeterminate color.

All the windows of the Cadillac were down.

When Jim got out, he noticed a very old man slumped in the backseat behind the driver's side, eyes wide open. Jim had to look twice to determine that the man was alive, then nodded to him as he passed. For some reason, the man looked vaguely familiar. Jim got no response, but the powerful smell of cheap whiskey as he walked by almost cut short his breath.

Maybe whatever poison they were serving inside had somehow blinded the old fool and he'd managed to get outside and climb into the backseat and was now patiently waiting to die.

Jim moved on to the building. Even though it was late, there was a bright full moon overhead.

He ducked inside the screen door, let it bang shut, then waited a moment or two for his eyes to grow accustomed to the dim, smoky interior. He wore lightweight khaki slacks, a short-sleeved

Hawaiian shirt he'd owned for years and scuffed white tennis shoes without socks.

It was as dressed-up as he ever got in Interception City.

He looked the place over. A badly worn linoleum counter ran the length of the side wall to the left, serving as the bar. In front of it stood an assortment of mismatched chrome barstools.

There were less than a dozen people spread out at several tables and at the bar, drinking, talking and listening to the creaky strains of a country music tune Jim couldn't begin to identify. The source of the music was a large 1950's style jukebox that stood beside the unisex bathroom, the door to which was closed.

A single overhead fan cut sluggishly through the humid murky air, weakly exchanging stale air for hot and hot air for smoky.

The bartender and owner, Big Jeff himself, stood at the far end of the narrow counter, hunched over as he talked across to a tanned, attractive thirty-something woman who sat looking down into her beer.

The woman was Wendy's younger sister, Pam Jamison, and she was a whole other story in her own right.

She wore tight black jeans and a skimpy black halter top designed to show her cleavage (and her bare trim middle), her dishwater blonde hair pulled back from her face into a casual ponytail. Her lipstick was a too-bright red, but it managed to make her full, cupid's bow mouth look sexy and appealing, inviting, really, and the rest of her makeup was applied sparingly enough to compliment her natural good looks without overdoing it.

Jim headed in that direction.

He got a few looks, a nod, and a quick glance here and there that just as quickly was turned away. It had been a long while since he'd spent any time at *The Alligator Pit* and he hadn't missed it one bit. These were not people he considered to be his friends, although he knew almost every single one of them.

Big Jeff saw him coming and straightened.

He dropped his cigarette to the floor behind the counter, put it out with his foot. He then waited, without smiling. Pam Jamison, talking to herself it seemed, didn't even look up.

Jim walked up to the counter and with an easy grace slid onto the stool next to her. He gave Big Jeff a look, a nod.

"Mr. Starke," Welsher said, civil enough but without a trace of warmth.

He was a good-sized man, thick in the middle but not soft, late fifties, with a bad haircut he might have paid a dollar for or got for free. He also had a face that had taken its share of abuse. His left eyebrow was neatly cut in two by a thick scar he'd take to the grave, the eye under it permanently half-closed.

He'd been a club fighter over in Miami once, and a mean-spirited street fighter, too, but not a particularly good one.

His real claim to fame, at least in his own mind, was that he was Police Chief Orville Goody's best friend. That bought him a lot in I.C., that longtime friendship with corrupt local authority, a lot of good will and quite a few benefits.

Benefits both legal and illegal.

"Drinking again, Jimmy?" he asked.

"I'll be sure to let you know when I start," Jim said. "Club soda on ice." To the woman next to him, he asked, "Buy you a beer, Pam?"

At this, Wendy's sister finally looked up with surprise from her drink, realizing someone had joined her. Her wide blue eyes narrowing, she took in Jim but clearly didn't like what she saw. It was immediately obvious she was already plenty drunk enough to be passed out cold, but for some reason she wasn't.

She apparently had energy to spare, even after midnight and seven or eight beers, her usual.

"Fuck you. . .fucker," she said slowly.

"Right," Jim shook his head. "You're not working here tonight?"

She gave him a look.

"Yeah, Big Jeff lets me sit at the bar drinking on the nights I work." She shook her head with disgust. "What do you want?" she managed. "Let me guess—it's something to do with my sister Wendy coming back this weekend for the big high school reunion, right?"

"Something like that," Jim admitted.

So Wendy *was* coming home.

Pam looked at him with unconcealed contempt, then turned away, ending the conversation. Jim Starke, of course, wasn't about to give up that easily.

"So, how about that beer?"

Her eyes, suddenly uncertain, flicked to Big Jeff, almost as if for approval. The man looked away, disgusted. He clearly *liked* her.

"So big deal," she finally said to Jim. "Buy me a damn beer."

And she downed the remains of the one in front of her, pushed across the glass to Big Jeff. He picked up the glass and walked away without a word. Jim tried a smile. Pam turned away again.

"So how are you doing?" he asked. "Anything exciting going on?"

She gave him a short humorless laugh.

"Right, lots of exciting stuff, every damn day."

She turned back to Jim, studied his expression, his face, as if searching for something. Their eyes met, held for a long moment. Her eyes were deeply blue, much like her sister's, but prolonged despair (and serious crying spells over her disappointing life) caused them to seem much older.

Then she turned back away and exhaled slowly.

She fished a cigarette out of a fake leopard-skin holder on the counter, snapped it shut, picked up the yellow Bic lighter next to it and lit it.

She didn't look back at him.

The past was past, and she was apparently smart enough to know it. That was clear, if nothing else was.

"I thought we ended up pretty good friends," he said. "Last time. . ."

"Yeah, right, you'll be coming back over one day to cut the lawn, wash the car and everything else..."

She shook her head again.

He thought she was suddenly on the verge of bursting into tears, and prayed she wouldn't; it'd be better if she just smacked him. Again. She'd done it before, long ago, and he'd just taken it. Rightly so.

Sitting there next to her, he suddenly felt as lousy as he'd ever remembered feeling, which could be plenty lousy.

He found himself needing a drink, a rum and Coke maybe, something sweet but strong, nothing that would taste much like a real drink, but at the same time he found it easy enough to resist.

Alcohol wasn't something he particularly craved.

Using her plastic lighter, he lit a cigarette instead, his first of the new day (or night), before he turned back to Pam.

Years ago, a few months after her older sister Wendy had run off to the big city of Orlando, seventeen-year-old I.C. High School senior Pam Jamison and expelled-during-his-last-year Jim Starke had become an item for a short time.

She'd had a crush on him for years, it turned out, but when he was dramatically thrown out of school just weeks before his own graduation, Pam flipped the rest of the way, the rebellious act that got him terminated from the world of formal education a wild young school girl's ultimate aphrodisiac:

He and Thurman Jr. had inserted a cherry bomb fuse into a lit cigarette in one of the boys' restrooms, not to damage the plumbing but just for laughs—and to hear how *loud* it'd be in such a tiled enclosure. From outside of the restroom, of course. Great fun.

Instead, they'd partially deafened a much-disliked male teacher who happened to see them acting suspiciously as they walked out, and wandered into the boys' restroom at exactly the wrong time to take a look.

After that, Pam *had* to have him.

That summer, she'd waited patiently (until her big sister was long-gone) for her chance at Jim.

And sometime during her following semester, she pounced, a vision of rampant hot teen sex in frosted-blonde hair, black lipstick, skimpy bra-less halters and miniscule short-shorts without underwear.

Her every move had been calculated to give him a peek in here and another up there, until, finally, she had her way with him.

She looked somewhat like Wendy, she sounded somewhat like Wendy, but Jim felt none of the paralysis that Wendy instilled in him, none of the hesitation, and they rolled into bed (or at least the cluttered back seat of his old car) on their first date, dinner at the *Countryside Diner* in Clewiston and almost a drive-in movie.

Though still a teen, Pam was no virgin.

And they were a natural, it seemed.

In fact, they were unable to keep their hands off each other, until finally, he one night came to fully realize she wasn't Wendy and never would be. That part would've been fine, had he merely kept his mouth shut, but he'd been stupid enough (think: *young* enough) to tell Pam it was only Wendy he was thinking of.

He'd given in to the '*need to confess...*' trait that many people (mostly decent folks) were afflicted with, a self-defeating attribute he'd long since overcome, but a little too late for his and Pam's so-called relationship to survive.

Their ending had been bitter.

They'd lasted a little over two months, then split up over two quick days, right in the middle of Pam's high school mid-terms. Breaking up with Jim Starke so demoralized the girl, in fact, that Pam Jamison immediately dropped out of high school and—even though Jim tried to stop her—still considered it *his* fault her life was over.

Of course, she was probably right, he'd often thought. It *was* his fault.

Chapter 15

Big Jeff brought back a draft beer and a club soda on ice, set down both glasses, then looked to Jim with open disapproval.

Jim paid him, told him to keep the change and met his gaze pointedly until the older man walked away.

Over the years, and possibly for no other reasons than intense sexual-chemistry, proximity and (when he was drinking) alcohol, Jim and Pam Jamison formed the unhealthy habit of falling into bed every now and then.

Ferociously into bed.

Followed, relentlessly, by unbridled regrets and recrimination, mainly on Pam's part, until Jim (almost three years earlier) finally managed to stop coming around. At least, for the wanton sex part.

For a time, he and Pam even became *almost* friends, able to stand each other without pawing each other, but then *that* didn't last all that long, either, and they just flat-out stopped talking.

At least, stopped talking in any way approaching civility. The woman's anger was apparently too great.

Of course, Pam's anger wasn't directed solely at Jim.

She didn't have much use for her sister Wendy either, although they hadn't seen each other in years. She'd many times let Jim know that her infrequent communications with Wendy, whether postcards, letters or even phone calls, were brief, uneventful, and without anything really said at all.

And no, no, and again no, Pam told him over the years, his name had never once come up.

* * *

Pam downed half the beer Jim had bought for her in one long swallow, then turned back to him.

"Look, you and my sister Wendy can go fuck yourselves," she started. "If she'll even talk to you when she gets here. She's coming back, but it doesn't have anything to do with you *or* me. Just stay the hell out of my life, both of you."

And she looked at him for a long moment, waiting for him to possibly say something reassuring or even. . . comforting perhaps, but Jim Starke had run out of reassuring and comforting words years ago.

He just stared back at her.

"Go away," she finally said.

Jim nodded, sorry at that moment that he'd even bothered her. He should have known better.

"Is there a problem here?" someone large and clearly unfriendly loomed to Jim's right. "This bastard still bothering you, Pam?"

From where he sat, Jim slowly turned to look up at the extremely large bulk of Sherman Anderson, Pam and Wendy Jamison's first cousin and Pam's sometime-boyfriend.

Anderson apparently had been in the restroom a very long time; most likely it had to do with illicit drugs.

Although he'd started on steroids while on the varsity football team at about the same time Jim Starke left I.C. High, Sherman Anderson had quickly graduated to other, darker, street pharmaceuticals in the pursuit of more strength, more speed and an overall better lifestyle.

It didn't seem to be working, even after all these years.

"I told you before, Starke, stay away from my cousin. She don't need any more of your bullshit."

"Hey, Anderson," Jim said. "Buy you a drink?"

Sherman Anderson was the same age as Jim, but his baby-like face and doughy white complexion made him somehow seem years younger. With no chin to speak of, smallish ears that laid back flat against his large head and a bristly short haircut, his clean-shaven face appeared so round it was as if a child had drawn it with a pencil and compass.

In fact, except for his pure bulk, he looked anything but dangerous—and yet, in truth, he very much was.

When he got no response, Jim added:

"I was just leaving."

But as he slid off the stool, Sherman Anderson stepped closer. A bit too close, actually, and then the bigger man didn't move, standing nose-to-nose with Jim but several times wider.

So Jim moved to step around Anderson.

But the much larger man silently shifted his considerable bulk to the side, muscles bulging under a sweaty white tee-shirt and several accumulated layers of fat, blocking Jim's path again, his expression sullen with apparent pent-up rage, his jealousy clearly so great he couldn't get even another word out.

His round face was much redder than usual, his breathing harsh, the sweaty smell of him overly apparent.

Off to the far side, Jim could tell that Big Jeff and most of the bar had suddenly quieted down, attuned to the potential for some serious one-on-one violence that probably wouldn't end well.

It was a crowd that liked blood.

"I don't see your good ol' buddy Thurman Jr. around," Anderson finally said. "I guess that boy knows better than to come in here when I'm around."

That got everybody's attention.

"Jesus, *Sherman*. . *!*" Pam cut in, standing suddenly.

Saying something like *that* about Thurman Jr., in a place where it might actually get back to the man, was a very good way to die. Or, at the very least, get broken up into many pieces.

Pam grabbed her cousin's meaty arm, her fingers digging so hard into the white flesh it left marks. She told him, "The old man's out in the car and it's time we got him home."

Jim Starke said nothing.

But he suddenly realized the old white-haired fool paralyzed with drink in the beat-to-shit Cadillac outside was Wendy and Pam's father, Cuthbert Jamison, a crotchety old bastard who had disliked, no, *hated* Jim Starke from the start.

No wonder he'd looked familiar, although it'd been many long years since Jim had last seen him.

Sherman Anderson shook Wendy's hand loose like a petulant child and stood his ground.

"I'm not afraid of this bastard, like the rest of these idiots...*or* of that psycho Thurman Jr..."

Jim suddenly knew it was definitely going to start.

"Anderson. . ." Jim Starke began, reasonably. "I've got nothing against you, chicken-fucking steroid redneck asshole that you are—"

And at the same moment he snapped a very quick right straight into Anderson's nose, the simplest thing he knew to do.

It was high school, but it worked.

The bigger man did not go down, or even fall back, nor did Jim Starke expect him to, but he immediately turned around and grabbed his face with both hands, a cry of huge pain escaping him.

Blood gushed between Anderson's thick white fingers, surprising and scaring the big man even more, a fountain of it from what Jim could see.

Pam was again beside her cousin in an instant, trying to help, trying to see.

He brushed her away, blood everywhere, the floor suddenly wet with it, the shock of the pain overwhelmingly intense as Sherman Anderson haltingly tried to catch his breath.

"Damn you, Jim," Pam hissed. "What the hell are you doing?!"

He gave her an incredulous look.

"Pam, look at the size of him—he'd have broken me in two!"

The other folks in the bar, Big Jeff included, continued to watch, alert for any sudden moves or surprise lunges on Anderson's part, maybe just a steamroller attack or a broken bottle or hidden knife, to make things right, to even the score, but none was forthcoming.

In truth, that single squarely thrown punch had broken the cartilage in the bridge of Anderson's nose and given the big man an instantaneous headache, neck-ache and jaw-ache that couldn't be ignored.

"I didn't want to hurt him," Jim added.

He picked up his cigarettes off the counter, stuffed them into the pocket of his Hawaiian shirt.

"This isn't the end of it," Anderson managed to burble through his own blood, still not looking up.

"If I ever see you anywhere near either Pam or Wendy. . ."

Jim studied him a long moment, then just shook his head.

Terrific, he thought, as he headed for the door.

Chapter 16

Stepping into his darkened trailer, the first thing Jim Starke noticed was the tiny range light he always left on over the built-in Amana had again burned out.

He worked his way across the small kitchen in the dark, then cursed when he stumbled over one of his two metal folding chairs sticking out into the room. He kicked the damn chair completely over, reached up and flipped the switch on the range hood to make certain the light was really out, but then was surprised (if only for a scant second) when the narrow greasy light flicked on.

He knew instantly he wasn't alone.

He flipped off the switch just as quickly, dropped silently in the dark to the floor in front of the stove. He listened intently, but heard nothing. Then he slid over in front of the refrigerator.

The refrigerator light had been unscrewed so Jim could get out the H&K .45 without making himself the most lit-up object (target!) in the room.

He pulled open the door, reached into the cold lower crisper drawer under the oranges and silently slipped out the gun.

His eyes grew quickly accustomed to the dark.

"If you're looking for something to steal," he announced, "there's nothing here to take."

"No shit," Thurman Jr. said from the darkness of the front room. "I couldn't even find enough to make a goddamn sandwich."

Jim relaxed his grip on the gun, sat down fully on the thin linoleum floor. He could suddenly smell his own sweat. He exhaled slowly.

"Thurman, I should just shoot you anyway."

"Please don't kill me, Mr. Homeowner," his friend said. "I've got way too much to live for."

Jim laughed without humor.

"Don't we both," he said.

He finally stood up, flipped the tiny range hood light back on, then returned the H&K .45 to the lower crisper drawer. The light did almost nothing to brighten up the kitchen or the living room, instead only dimly lit the small surface of the gas stove itself. He didn't bother turning on another light.

He up-righted the metal folding chair he'd kicked over and slid it under the scarred Formica table jutting out from the wall, directly across from the matching one.

"Why are you sitting in the dark?" Jim wanted to know, looking down to the large man sitting in shadow at the far end of the couch.

"Too damn bright."

Thurman Jr. was drinking directly from a quart bottle of 'Orange Driver,' a concoction of sticky commercial orange drink and cheap vodka sold at his store. It was a big seller. He began squeezing a heavy, spring-loaded grip strengthener in his free hand, with a nerve-grating intensity.

Jim got out his cigarettes, found matches in a drawer, lit his second one of the night. He threw the match in the sink, his cigarettes on the counter.

"What's going on?"

"My mother didn't come home tonight," Thurman Jr. said. "My dad called the store worried to death. Did you see Edna June today?"

Jim took a drag off his cigarette.

"Edna June's still not home at 3:00 A.M.?"

Thurman Jr. paused in his drinking to give him a look.

"Damn her ass," the larger man exhaled. "If it's some other guy again, I'll kill the son of a bitch. I mean it. The old man's just that—too damn old to take this kind of shit anymore."

He switched the grip strengthener to his right hand, continued squeezing it without pause, now a big mean cricket with an even nastier attitude, his expression suddenly unreadable as he nodded to himself about some inner thought he apparently wasn't about to share.

The metallic spring sound gradually took on the nature of a warning somehow, to Jim at least, as if a time bomb was steadily clicking along, ticking along, on its way to an inevitable—and very bad—end.

"I don't get it. Where could she be?"

Where was she?

Edna June was going straight home, or so he thought, after leaving his trailer, and had been in a big hurry to do so. Christ, that was over *seven* hours ago. . .

Thurman Jr. shook his head with disgust. He finally tossed aside the spring-loaded grip strengthener.

"If she knows what's good for her, she'd better be dead."

His idea of humor. Jim said nothing.

There was a long silence as both men considered the situation. It became a *very* long silence. Finally, Jim said:

"Wendy's coming back for the reunion."

"The lost love of your life—"

"Yeah."

Jim shook his head at the thought.

"Love's fucked, you know," Thurman Jr. said. "Everything my mother's put my father through taught me that. And the old man just takes it..." He took a long drink. "The dumb fuck."

He finished the bottle of Orange Driver, upending it to the get the last swallow, then with his free hand absently found *something* wedged in between Jim's couch cushions. Jim watched—suddenly wondering if the man might come up with some part of Edna June's intimate apparel or some other, possibly identifiable, object she owned—but relaxed when a 9mm Glock 17 appeared in his hand.

"Jesus, you *are* worried about burglars!" his friend said.

"I forgot that was in there."

Thurman Jr. hefted the dark gray gun, then sighted down the barrel just to the right of Jim's head. "Good thing it was me, not somebody with a reason to kill you."

"Yeah, good thing," Jim agreed. "So, did you call the police about Edna June?"

Thurman Jr. gave him a look before he put down the Glock.

"The I.C. Police?"

"Well. . .that's where we live."

"Chief Orville Goody couldn't find his dick in the dark with a flashlight and a search party," the big man said. True enough. "My dad called earlier—nothing. And ever since Edna June tried to get the crooked bastard fired, he doesn't much like us."

This was also true.

"Right," Jim agreed. "But if it's an accident or something, we need to find out about it. Maybe we should drive around, see what we can see…."

Thurman Jr. stood up suddenly.

"Yeah, maybe we'll spot her SUV is some asshole's driveway. I'd love to punch the living shit out of somebody about now."

He picked up the Glock 17 again.

"On second thought—"

"Perfect," Jim said.

Chapter 17

In a remote section of pure swamp seven miles outside of Interception City, Edna June Thurman's large black Toyota FJ Cruiser raced at gathering speed through the jungle. It followed a narrow beaten-down dirt path for fifty feet off the road before the large vehicle effectively ended its existence by slamming head-on into a huge cypress tree.

The tree didn't budge. The vehicle's engine continued to race, a broken chunk of driftwood wedged onto the accelerator.

Several long moments later, Officer Ray peered into the SUV through the shattered driver-side window, ignoring the dead black man slumped behind the wheel. Across the console, he could see Edna June's crumpled shape lying half-on and half-off the passenger seat.

He nodded to himself, then tossed a makeshift burning torch into the back seat. The torch landed next to several plastic gallon milk jugs filled with gasoline.

Officer Ray barely got his face back out of the way before it all went up in a huge fireball.

"Jesus!" he gasped, trying to catch his breath.

While the vehicle brightly burned at the base of the tree, he stood next to Chief Goody, his father-in-law clearly not pleased with the most recent criminal adventure the other man had gotten him into.

There'd been a few, over the years.

Finally, Chief Goody gave him a sour look.

"Why isn't the gas tank going up?"

"It will, don't worry."

"Don't worry?" the Chief said. "You stupid son of a bitch, why the hell'd I listen to you? The swamp's here for a reason. People disappear in it all the time, cars, too." He fixed the other man with a baleful look. "I got a bad feeling about this."

"They'll be no evidence left, just twisted metal and burned up ashes—"

Officer Ray was cut off when Edna June Thurman suddenly sat up in the passenger seat of the hugely burning vehicle, screaming over the roar of the fire. She flailed about helplessly but couldn't get out.

Officer Ray, for all his petty meanness and cruel nature, was nonetheless shocked. He looked to the Chief.

"You said you choked her!"

Chief Orville Goody, knowing full well that Edna June had still been alive, said simply, "She deserves this."

* * *

Jim and Thurman Jr. turned a downtown corner in Jim's CJ-5 Jeep. Miles away, they suddenly saw a fire that dimly lit up the sky above the trees. From their vantage point, it looked like a serious one.

"Another damn fire in the swamp ," the bigger man said. "Some fucking alligator poacher probably."

Jim didn't agree.

"Lightning."

To which Thurman Jr. pointed out, "It's a bright moon, no clouds."

"Clear sky lightening," Jim said. "You don't need clouds for lightning in Florida. This is a place you can get killed anytime, anywhere."

"True enough..."

Chapter 18

Virginia Lanyard (known online as Virgin69_4U) sat at her desktop computer in her bedroom on a hardback chair fitted with a homemade navy blue corduroy cushion. She was in skimpy cut-off shorts and a string bikini top, sat watching herself in the narrow full-length mirror on the back of the bedroom door.

The mirror was slightly warped, by age, by cheap workmanship, by the unrelenting heat that permeated the narrow trailer, and it gave her already skinny frame an even skinnier, more angular cast.

Virginia didn't mind, though, because she knew she looked good in real life—she just liked to watch herself get sexy. Which was what she mostly did whenever she was on her computer.

Untouched by the sun, she was impossibly pale for a Florida girl, her white skin so perfect it was almost translucent, her wild black curly hair, worn fairly short and parted in the center, startling in its contrast to her angelic face.

She was a naturally pretty girl, anyway, with finely chiseled features, deeply inquisitive dark brown eyes behind large, bookworm-like glasses (which gave her a schoolgirl look that she cultivated, especially when on her webcam), and a captivating mouth she knew got its share of attention.

Every boy and man around town had noticed her over the last couple of years, but each had had to think twice about doing anything about it— she was Police Chief Orville Goody's only daughter and now, worse (although she was still just 17-years-old), she'd become Officer Ray Lanyard's lawfully bedded wife, the skinny pervert bastard no doubt having his weird way with her every single night.

Virginia studied herself in the mirror, then smiled and looked back to her monitor. In truth, she was mostly and truly alive only on the Internet. Her actual life bored her to near-screaming tears.

Virgin69_4U had been web surfing for over two-and-a-half years, was offended by almost nothing, and was exceptionally adept at discovering both people and sites that amused her.

And aroused her.

It was after dark and she was waiting for her husband to get home.

Their older mobile home was situated so far back on a large parcel of partially-cleared land it was nearly invisible from the road, their long driveway snaking through a thick stand of tall underbrush and jungle. The place had been given to them by her parents and was free and clear.

Which was why, to her chagrin, they'd probably end up living there the rest of their lives. Virginia, of course, had always hoped she'd one day be living in a far larger city, one that could legitimately be called a *city*.

This was one of the reasons she spent so much time on the Internet, her only real escape from her boring, often dreary, reality.

* * *

The instant she heard Ray's unmarked patrol car turn off the highway and start up their long gravel driveway, she logged off.

Ray knew absolutely nothing about computers and couldn't even be tempted to sit at one. He did, however, know of her preoccupation with sexual matters, and encouraged it more often than not (as his fantasies involved many ideas from a collection of Florida swinger magazines he'd picked up over the years in Clewiston), but he had no idea concerning her nearly full-time online sexual escapades.

Virginia Lanyard heard his unmarked car hit the brakes as it reached the trailer in the dark—gravel flying in all directions, the damn fool idiot screeching up like his ass was on fire and she had the only hose.

What the hell was on the man's mind?

She clicked the Windows shut-down button and dashed as best she could for the bathroom so she could get re-composed in private.

Standing at the sink, she heard him come through the front door.

"You here?" Ray Lanyard said, a little too loudly.

He closed the front door, hard, behind him. Then she heard him walk through the living room. Anger in his steps.

"Virginia! You damn well better be!"

Now what the hell was the matter?

"Ray, what are you all nuts about?" she asked with genuine curiosity, coming out of the bathroom in her cut-off shorts and the string-like orange and white checkered bikini top that just barely covered her.

She was cleaning her glasses with a piece of toilet paper, which she threw behind her into the bathroom wastebasket.

"I missed you, sweetie," she added, at the same time putting back on those big black librarian glasses of hers. She thought they made her look sexy and she was absolutely right. "What's going on?"

She looked good enough to eat standing up and they both knew it.

Ray stood without moving in the hallway, studying his attractive young wife. It was obvious he liked what he saw but was also, for some unknown reason, angry as hell about some damn thing or another.

"What, Ray, what? Sane up, will you, and tell your sweetie pants what the big problem is."

And, with that, she headed back into the bedroom. There was absolutely nothing, she believed, that sooner or later couldn't be fixed in there.

He walked down the hallway but then stopped in the bedroom doorway, his hand on the butt of his holstered black Colt .45 semi-automatic like he was posing for a lawman of the year photo or something, staring after her, his black mirror sunglasses, 'Southern police-style' he called them, hanging from his right breast pocket.

His large black gun-belt was loaded with the tools of his trade: nightstick, Mace, radio, clips of bullets, all in black also, even his handcuffs, special order black alloy from a military supply store up in Orlando, all of it, somehow, looking just a bit too large for him.

He looked a little like the damn Terminator (if a much skinnier version) and that was exactly how he planned it.

"I had to kill a man today," Ray said finally.

"My God," Virginia moved to him in the doorway, uncertain, really, what the protocol here might be.

Her father, Police Chief Orville Goody, had supposedly killed several men in his years as a lawman, but he had never in his lifetime come home and mentioned it. It was a topic understood to be off limits to the family.

"Who and why?" she wanted to know.

My God, she thought, this *was* exciting.

"Friend of yours," her husband said. "From Orlando, was a nigger, had some pretty wild pictures of you naked and showing it all."

And Virginia Lanyard's heart stopped cold, her throat tightening so much she suddenly couldn't get a breath.

She squeaked, in fact, trying to take one, but was being strangled by an invisible hand, the same hand that a second later was squeezing her heart relentlessly, holding it, keeping it totally still, so that she was certain she was about to die, not by Ray, but just out of pure and simple guilt.

And fear.

Extremely great fear.

Chapter 19

"Ray?!" she barely managed, after a long silence. "Ray, are you crazy?!"

From his left unbuttoned breast pocket, her husband silently produced a handful of bare-assed pictures of Virginia that she knew with certainty Mr. Elmore Hightower had printed out of his own computer on photographic stock.

He tossed them at her bare feet.

"Ray, damn it, this is crazy!"

But she stooped down and scooped up the photos (less than a week ago scanned into her computer and sent to the man in Orlando), as she recognized each and every one but pretended to see them for the very first time.

Oh, Jesus, save me!

"Look familiar?" Ray asked.

"Ray, these are all pictures *you* took of me. How did they get into the hands of a black man from Orlando, do you think?"

Her husband stared at her in disbelief for a long moment.

"Jesus, Virginia," he said with a sudden weariness. "God, you are a slut-and-a-half, but the fuck of it is, I still love you!"

"And I love *you*, sweetheart!"

She smiled gamely.

Virginia knew her man, and she recognized the moment.

She pulled him the rest of the way into the bedroom and down onto their kingsized bed, quickly straddling him and then holding his gaze.

"Ray, I can explain everything," she breathed into his mouth, kissing him so hotly it was a miracle his bullets didn't explode. "It was supposed to be a surprise, but damn it, now you've gone and spoiled it all by killing the man!"

Officer Ray gave his teen bride a look.

"What the hell are you talking about?"

Still straddling him, Virginia leaned over to the nightstand on Ray's side of the bed and yanked open the flimsy drawer. It almost flew out on the floor, instead hung there precariously, as she rooted around through gun & ammo magazines, bullet clips, brass knuckles, two switch-blade knives, sap gloves, a blackjack, sugar-free gum and other assorted junk.

Finally she pulled out a well-thumbed copy of 'Florida Paradise – Swingers & Nudist Resort,' and shoved it in his face.

"We always look through this, talking about meeting some of these folks for a little fun, but we never *do* anything! I'm not complaining, all the sex we do is great, but, damn it, Ray, I was just taking the first real step!"

And Ray, shocked at the very idea, even though it was his own, said, "But those are *white* folks in there!"

"Not all of them."

He fixed her with a look.

"Damn it all to hell, Virginia, you know I can't stand blacks!"

"Ray…" she said with a little pout, as if this was all *his* fault that it'd finally come to this, "*you're* the one who wanted to try something different!"

"Not with black people! Virginia, are you crazy!? Let a black man into our marriage bed?"

"I was just going to talk to him…"

Officer Ray shook his head.

"It didn't sound like that on your call yesterday—on the tape I made."

She couldn't believe it.

If she'd had a cell phone, instead of that stupid landline her backwards hick of a redneck husband insisted on hanging onto, it would have *never* happened. Her getting taped. And caught.

"You taped my calls? Ray!"

He nodded with conviction.

"You been acting funny the last few days so I went over to Radio Shack in Clewiston—"

Virginia decided to change direction.

"Ray, what did any black people ever do to you?" she wanted to know. "You don't even *know* any black people. And neither do I. This isn't a city they tend to congregate in."

He gave her a smile.

"Thanks to your father and all his good work with the KKK over the years..."

"Ray, in your entire damn life, has a black person ever personally done anything to hurt you?" she continued. And, when he refused to answer, "It's all theory, your hating 'em and all, isn't it?"

"They come through here once in a while," Ray protested. "I've dealt with the blacks before, as the law."

"I'm sure," she said, suddenly imagining it. "I'll bet you're real nice to 'em, too."

"I treat 'em special, all right," he laughed.

But not pleasantly.

* * *

Walter Hightower was trapped in his unmarked car, in a miles long back-up on the southbound Turnpike heading towards Miami. And into the Florida Everglades. He exhaled slowly, ready to explode with the frustration of such a tie-up in the middle of the night.

Orange plastic barrels lining the side of the highway prevented him from simply racing down the shoulder.

The dispatcher on his radio told him, "Animal Control's scraping a dead squirrel off the right lane. It clears at exit 136, so it must be gawkers."

Walter shook his head.

"Miles of morons. I can't believe I'm sitting here with a loaded gun and not doing something about it."

He heard a short laugh from the radio.

"I didn't hear that, Walter."

* * *

"But damn you, Ray, why did you have to kill him?!" Virginia asked. "He didn't do a damn thing, and now you're going to jail!"

Her husband gave her a shrug, lying beside her.

His hot young wife had just humped his brains out, using all her substantial naked youthful charms to make him go even a second time right away, not their usual thing, tiring him out, wearing him out, *wringing* him out, he admitted, but only to himself. Not to her.

Never to her.

He'd *never* admit to Virginia that she was absolutely *too* much for him. Sexually, that is. Because he knew, if she had her way, she'd go all night and all day and then some more.

Not that he'd ever complain.

Rather, he'd keep up with the girl as best he could even if it literally killed him one long night. Not a bad way to go, after all, but it *was* a serious strain, him being a much older man.

"I didn't even know your man was a black until I pulled him over outside of town in that black sports car he mentioned on the phone." Ray shook his head, grimaced at the thought. "When I realized this black bastard was the one, I just went crazy and shot him."

"Oh, God, I don't believe this."

He gave her his most serious look.

"Here's a full-grown black adult, male, coming to our peaceful little city to sex up my sweet young teenage wife and you ask why I shot him?"

"Ray, they got the electric chair in this state!"

He just shook his head.

"It's mostly lethal injection these days."

"Well, okay, everything's fine then…"

But then Ray looked back to her with a weird little smile.

"I called your daddy," he said. "Everything *is* fine."

"It's not funny! You killed a real person."

Officer Ray just shook his head again.

"He had to be wanted," he told her. "He had a big .44 under the seat, probably killed himself a liquor store clerk somewhere, was on the run—"

Virginia stared at him a long moment.

Then she said, "He wasn't like that."

"Yeah, right—"

She swallowed hard and added, "He said it was a secret, but he was an undercover man for the Florida Department of Law Enforcement, heading down to Key West on a big drug bust…"

And with that, Officer Ray Lanyard blinked and suddenly just stared at her.

Chapter 20

"Good goddamn!" Police Chief Orville Goody swore, reaching over to his nightstand for the ringing phone that had just awakened him. "Now what the hell?"

It was very early Saturday morning, a little before 6:00 A.M., not a civilized hour to be up as far as the police chief was concerned (unless a man was still awake from the night before). Of course, he had well known what the call was about so he wasn't as irritated as he pretended.

His act of surprise, in fact, was solely for the benefit of his wife, Brenda Marie (B.M. to her friends, but only the really close ones; everyone else kind of snickered when they heard it, really pissing her off).

She raised her head up slightly, but only slightly, to hear what was going on this time of the morning, serious trouble for sure if anyone from the department was bothering the police chief at home.

Brenda Marie was a big woman, just like Orville Goody was a big man, and it had surprised them both when Virginia—their sweet little angel—had grown up so skinny and petite and perfect.

"Well, what is it?" the wife demanded, her broad face devoid of makeup and virtually disappearing even as he glanced over at her. She was all white skin, pale freckles and even paler eyebrows and eyelashes, almost invisible in the morning, in fact, before she painted on her daytime face. "Orville. . !"

He continued to look at her, holding the phone out; whoever was on the other end had to hear him say:

"I ain't even answered the goddamn thing!"

Brenda Marie did not flinch, or even blink, just silently glared right back with mean little blue-gray eyes so pale they were almost colorless, or translucent, actually.

One of these fine days. . .he thought to himself. Then:

"Go ahead," he said finally into the mouthpiece. And then, "Jesus Christ! You're sure it's her? Damn, this'll be trouble for sure. I'll meet you there."

And he hung up the phone and lay back for a long moment, his large head resting on his pillow, still waking up basically, but enjoying keeping the little lady (no longer little, not ever little really, even when they first married) in real suspense.

"So what *is* it?" Brenda Marie insisted. "Damn you, Orville Goody—"

He let her wait another long moment, then informed her, "That idiot woman Edna June Thurman got herself killed last night, off County Road 823, hit a big damn cypress tree taking a corner too fast, car burned up with her in it."

Brenda Marie was suddenly sitting up in bed.

"Oh, my God Almighty," she gasped, shocked to the core of her solid one hundred and eighty-five pound frame. "That's terrible."

And she crossed herself.

Police Chief Goody hauled his big ass out of bed, lazily scratched himself front and back through his baggy undershorts, then stood up. He headed for the bathroom, didn't bother turning the light on. He didn't plan on cleaning up too much anyway.

He knew it'd be better if he showed up unshaved and uncombed, like he just jumped up and rushed off, so shocked was he by the whole damn thing.

"Not the worst of it," he told his wife from the toilet, through the open door. "Was someone else driving, unknown male, not the mister. John Pasco said she had her face in his lap, orally servicing him, it looked like, probably lost control when she finally satisfied him."

Brenda Marie was beyond being merely shocked at this point.

"My God in Heaven!" she gasped again. "Officer Pasco said all *that* in the two seconds you talked to him!?"

The Police Chief shook his head, reminded himself once again the missus wasn't as dumb as he often presumed she was. "Pasco's a damn fast talker when he needs to be. Said he thought it was a nigger, couldn't tell exactly with both burned up so bad, but he thought so anyway."

This last was entirely too much for Brenda Marie.

Her head felt like it was ready to literally explode. She suddenly realized she was shaking.

"You're saying our high school vice principal, Mrs. Edna June Thurman, got herself killed providing oral sex to an unknown black man?"

Finished on the toilet, Police Chief Goody wiped and flushed.

He stood up, pulled up his shorts, didn't bother washing his hands and then walked back out into the bedroom. In the lessening near dark of the coming morning sun through the shade, he picked up his uniform pants off the back of the chair where he'd tossed them the night before.

They would do.

"That's right," he told his wife. He started pulling on his pants. "And yet ignorant people with no actual experience keep right on saying it ain't dangerous to mix the races."

Chapter 21

The lonely spot on County Road 823 commonly known as *Look Out Point* was as swampy and boring a stretch of two-lane asphalt as existed anywhere within the county, or within the entire state of Florida, for that matter.

Just north of Interception City, its colorful designation came not from any spectacular view, for the short low-lying stretch of road offered nothing more to see than an endless wall of trees and jungle-like underbrush only a foot or two off the shoulder. Rather, it was the "Look Out!" aspect of a surprising hairpin turn, following a graceful curve leading into it (and concealing its potentially deadly nature), after miles of pure straight monotony that caused it to be named so.

Over the years, many small but elaborate and varied crosses had appeared, memorials to dozing, drinking, inattentive or speeding drivers who had not survived the turn, even with the new road signs in place.

Citing the dangers of obstructed views, a roadside distraction and the occasional grieving family that spilled out onto the roadway, the county routinely removed the crosses after a suitable period had passed. Had they not been removed, twenty-three such memorial crosses to date would decorate the landscape.

As it was, only two, less than one hundred feet from one another, stood as a somber reminder of the carnage the short stretch of bloody road had seen.

By 6:35 A.M. on Saturday, Look Out Point was once again packed solid with every I.C. police car, fire engine, ambulance, road maintenance crew pick-up, wrecker, flatbed and any other automobile or truck with flashing lights on top that was available throughout the county.

It was an event.

A roadblock had been set up, orange flashing barricades keeping the merely curious at a distance, although at this time of morning no curious had as yet arrived. Not even the press had appeared, although they were certain to storm the location as soon as they heard what was going on.

More than one 'unnamed source' within the Interception City Police Department, working for the most meager of unofficial stipends—usually just a quick lunch or a six-pack—had undoubtedly raced to get on their cell phones right after arriving at the scene.

The center of attention, barely visible from behind the line of barricades, was Edna June

Thurman's burned-out black Toyota FJ Cruiser. It sat still smoldering, the front of it crushed nearly beyond recognition as if merely a flattened beer can, the large 4-wheel-drive vehicle apparently driven head-on into the huge cypress tree without any attempt to stop.

Two firemen trained a single hose from the fire engine onto the wreck, soaking it thoroughly so it wouldn't surprise anyone by bursting into flames again.

The Toyota FJ Cruiser's trajectory off the road, straight back to the tree from the dead center of the hairpin turn without slowing down, was easily reconstructed along the narrow path of battered and broken tropical brush. The tremendous impact had caused several darkly tinted windows in the vehicle to explode. For 10 yards in every direction a ragged circle of black surrounded the scorched tree, the lush underbrush charred into ash from the heat.

Only a solid month of torrential rains, tapering off finally in the last day or two, had kept the entire woods from going straight up. That and the odd fact that the fire seemed to have been centered in the *interior* of the vehicle, as if the seats themselves had suddenly burst into flames, rather than the gas tank itself.

Back at the barricades, the first member of the press to arrive, Charlie 'Buzz' Jordan, the nightly news anchor and on-the-road-man from Channel 62 over in Wanderly, was already into an argument with his own brother, Billy Jordan, an I.C. police officer manning his post.

Billy had instructions to gut-shoot, if necessary, any media types trying to get in.

Until Police Chief Orville Goody and Mayor George Elliot themselves had a chance to get together and put everything into proper perspective, no one, period, was to talk to the press.

"Well, just tell me if the Mayor's even here yet," Buzz wanted to know, trying to see past his own damn brother, but I.C. Officer Billy Jordan, taller and wider, kept moving slightly in whatever direction Buzz's glance seemed to go, effectively keeping the man from seeing any damn thing in the woods at all.

Some kind of bad wreck was in there, that was certain, but why all the big to-do?

"Billy, I swear to Christ, you're no longer Chrissie's godfather, you're being such a damn jerk."

"Orders," was all Billy would say, repeating it, like one of those foreign palace guards who wasn't allowed to smile, talk or do anything to jeopardize his post. He shrugged again. "From the Chief himself. Orders."

In truth, Billy's 'big-time TV newsman' brother often irritated the hell out of him, lording it over the rest of the family like he did, and Billy was pleased, for once, for the opportunity to return the attitude.

Buzz looked over then, and tapped his bored young cameraman on the shoulder to follow quickly, when another section of the barricade was lifted out of the way by an I.C. police officer farther down the line.

The other officer was letting in an older dark blue Buick Park Avenue, followed closely by an even older bright red Jeep CJ-5 without doors or a top, both vehicles moving ahead so slowly it almost seemed as if their tires were somehow melting into the road.

Buzz and his cameraman got there just as the section of barricade was put back into place.

"Who was that?" Buzz quietly asked I.C. Officer Carl Ledbetter, his best kept secret source, in fact. "Carl . . ?"

Officer Ledbetter, first covertly looking around to make certain he wasn't being overheard, said out of the side of his mouth without glancing at Buzz:

"That was Mr. Horace Thurman Sr., his son, Thurman Jr., and the Jim Starke boy behind in the red Jeep. Looks like Mrs. Edna June Thurman finally got a mouthful she couldn't swallow."

Buzz nodded, but he didn't get it, not at all.

He looked to his cameraman to see if *he* got it, but the younger man, tired of standing around lugging the big Sony Betacam and wanting to get on with it, just shook his head.

Buzz turned back to Ledbetter.

"Carl, what the hell are you talking about?"

Chapter 22

This early Saturday morning scene at Look Out Point was what Wendy Jamison-Johnson and her daughter Jennifer, in Wendy's big gray Lincoln, came upon as they headed to Interception City.

Wendy had cut off the main road south, U.S. 27, just northwest of Clewiston and taken CR 823 for many miles through the middle of nowhere, as they say, knowing it would eventually lead directly into downtown I.C., located even *farther* in the middle of absolutely nowhere.

At least that was the plan.

Her blonde 14-year-old daughter was half-asleep, restlessly so, slumped into her corner against the door, her head pressed into the pillow she'd brought along. No way was she sleeping on any articles of bedding provided by anyone within her mother's (and by extension, her *own*) horrible family!

No thanks.

The sky was crystal clear directly above them, flawless blue without a cloud or even a hint of one in sight, but off to the far east, towards the Atlantic Ocean where the sun was rising, it was apparent a morning storm was picking up strength.

Towering black thunderheads were building fast, stretching along the horizon as far as the eye could see, sunlight shooting through them and turning the sky in that direction into colors as vivid and darkly crimson as dried blood.

"What's this?" Wendy said, slowing at the first sight of the many flashing lights. "Is it a huge accident?"

"Who cares?" Jennifer said groggily. She was trying to get more comfortable, wedged into her corner and pushing her pillow around, but wasn't having very much luck. "Wake me up when it's time to head back home."

Such had been the tone of the entire trip, whenever the girl deigned to speak to her mother at all. She was still furious about being dragged to hell and back, if they *did* get back, which she was highly doubtful about.

"Quiet," Wendy said, stopping at the barricade. "This looks serious."

Jennifer chose to ignore her, which was fine with Wendy.

She was tired of her daughter's attitude, the girl not even trying to understand her mother's side of it. Had she been willing to communicate a little, Wendy believed, it might have done both of them a lot of good, might have definitely made the weekend trip itself more worthwhile.

As it was, Wendy was thinking the entire idea was making less and less sense and she was half-tempted to just turn right around and head back to Orlando. Springing such a potentially unpleasant surprise upon an already seriously angry 14-year-old suddenly seemed less and less necessary.

What the hell, she was beginning to wonder, had she been thinking?

And then, as she sat at the barricade, flashing lights in every direction yet no indication what was going on, a good-looking policeman was tapping at her window politely.

"What's going on, Officer?" she rolled down her window.

And Jennifer finally opened her eyes and sat up.

She looked around like a just-born puppy, more curious than she was willing to admit, but as seemingly blasé as possible about the whole situation.

As far as she was concerned, clearly, the entire population of Interception City, men, women, children and even pets, could be dead out there, flattened in the middle of the road, and she couldn't have cared less.

In fact, she preferred that *would* be the case. Then they could just turn right around and head back home.

"Big accident, in the woods there," the policeman said. And then, "Hey, I'm Billy Jordan, from I.C. High....aren't you Wendy Jamison?"

And at that, Jennifer suddenly exhaled loudly and rolled her big blue eyes with clear annoyance.

My God, they were already meeting her mom's awful friends...

Chapter 23

Police Chief Orville Goody and Officer Ray Lanyard stood back from the blackened vehicle in the wooded near-darkness of early morning, watching the firemen continue to hose it down. They were waiting for the mayor to haul his skinny ass out of bed and get out to the site so they could move forward on this thing.

It wasn't that Mayor Elliot was part of any official police action or anything, but past experience taught the Chief to include the mayor in any serious activity, positive or negative, that went on in his domain.

George Elliott wasn't the most understanding of souls and this was sure to raise some unpleasant questions.

Standing about twenty yards away, Chief Goody noted, silently watching also, was the Thurman family, Horace Thurman Sr., of course, and Thurman Jr. and their close friend, Jim Starke, none of them looking at all happy.

"That gas tank didn't finish the job," Chief Goody pointed out to Officer Ray. "Looks like it just fizzled."

"I was sure it would go up," Ray said.

"Again, what the hell did I listen to you for? Jesus H. Christ, I must be getting senile..."

To which his son-in-law merely looked away sheepishly. The Chief shook his head, then looked back to what remained of the Thurman family.

Mr. Thurman had been called as soon as the license plate of the vehicle, badly burned but readable, had been called in by the reporting I.C. police officer, John Pasco.

Pasco had been called out to Look Out Point because of the fire.

Police Chief Goody, watching the Thurman group, was barely able to suppress a wide smile. Aside from the obvious political differences that had come up in last year's acrimonious attempt to replace him, he did *not* like the Thurman family anyway and was secretly very pleased at their misfortune.

He finally walked over to them.

"Mr. Thurman..." he nodded.

The elderly man looked up.

"Chief Goody."

"I thought you should know, there's an unknown black male behind the wheel. Mrs. Thurman's face apparently...uh...was in his lap." It let it sink in. "It really is a tragedy, two people dead, for whatever pointless reason."

Jim Starke studied Chief Goody for a long moment, but said nothing. Thurman Jr., likewise, did not appear to react to the news, but Mr. Thurman Sr. was visibly stunned by that unexpected information.

"What?" he got out. "A man was driving her car...?"

The police chief cleared his throat, shrugged as if it was information he was loathe to impart, but that it was also his sworn duty to report it.

And so report it he must.

"Well..."

Chapter 24

"Billy Jordan," Wendy smiled, astonished to see one of the genuine troublemakers she'd gone to I.C. High School with in uniform. "You're a police officer now?"

He beamed at the gorgeous blonde woman in the Lincoln.

"That I am," he told her. "I'm remembering all those times we were stuck in detention together."

"Right," she nodded slowly, preferring *not* to remember. Now that she was here, realizing she preferred not to remember *anything* about I.C. High, in fact. "So, what's going on up there? Is it an accident? Someone local?"

Officer Billy nodded, then looked back to the scene down the road.

"Remember Mrs. Thurman, in English and math…?"

And Wendy, shocked to the core by this information, glanced over to Jennifer to gauge her reaction but, of course, Jennifer merely stared back at her, puzzled.

The young girl had no idea who Edna June Thurman was.

* * *

Jim Starke watched as the two I.C. fire fighters finally turned off the water they'd been directing at the smoldering Toyota FJ Cruiser and started heading back to the fire engine.

It was time for the police to move in, and that's exactly what Orville Goody did, approaching the vehicle and escorting the Banyon County Coroner, the very young Doctor David Dennison (Dr. Death, behind his back), and elderly Mayor George Elliot, who had just arrived, to the scene.

Officer Ray Lanyard, standing alone out on the otherwise deserted road a quarter mile back—the rising damp heat of the coming day already causing him to perspire so profusely even his black Jockey underwear felt wet—had been instructed by the Police Chief to stay there and direct the flow of non-existent traffic.

The Mayor, who they'd all been waiting for, walked straight through, head down and watching where he was going, without noticing the Thurman family.

As horribly bad as Jim felt about Edna June Thurman's terrible but unaccountable death, he could only imagine the grief Horace Thurman Sr. and Thurman Jr. must have felt. The older

Thurman, tall, stooped, gray and in his late seventies, looked more to be in his nineties; over the years, he hadn't aged particularly well and the shock of Edna June's sudden demise was unlikely to help. He wore an expensive-looking hearing aid in his right ear, simple wire frame glasses, and a lightweight dark blue windbreaker even in the already oppressive early morning heat. The windbreaker hung on his sparse frame as if merely draping a narrow coat rack, so thin had he finally become. He held a balled-up handkerchief tightly in his hand.

"This isn't right," he kept saying, weakly but with conviction, over and over. His moist eyes were rimmed with red. He'd been silently crying, off and on, all morning. "This just isn't right."

And Jim Starke silently agreed with him, although he wasn't certain what aspect of the woman's death the man referred to: for her to pass on at a comparatively young age in relation to her older husband? Or to the unknown dead black man beside her, behind the wheel, apparently joined eternally in a common enough sexual activity while driving?

"It *isn't* right," Jim finally said aloud, to which Mr. Thurman turned to him as if just realizing he was there. "There's something very wrong here."

Thurman Jr., who hadn't uttered a word since arriving at the scene, looked to Jim as well, but said nothing. He was in faded jeans and an even more faded black tee shirt. His expression was blank, revealing nothing of his thoughts within. To

Jim's mind, it was more unnerving than had the big man showed something, anything, even violence, directed wherever, in reaction to his mother's unexpected death.

The night before, they had driven hell-bent all over I.C. in Jim's battered red jeep, crisscrossing back and forth, cutting down side streets and narrow dirt alleys, searching for a glimpse of Edna June's Toyota FJ Cruiser so that Thurman Jr. might burst in and beat the living shit out of someone, anyone, he caught with her.

Or even use the Glock.

But they hadn't found her. Of course, they never considered heading out this far into the country.

And, all night long, Jim Starke had kept expecting the woman to just show up eventually at the Thurman house, with God-only-knew what kind of crazy story or excuse, so that everything could get back to normal.

But it had never happened. And now it never would.

"Something's wrong here," he said still again.

What Jim meant, of course, without saying it, was there was no possible way in the wide, wide world that Edna June Thurman could end up out on CR 823, miles north from her straight path home from Jim's trailer park, dead in her burning Toyota FJ Cruiser with an unknown black lover.

It was ridiculous.

Had Edna June Thurman been heading to a secret black lover for a fast-moving fun time out in the country after leaving Jim's trailer, she'd have given him each and every particular, before *and* after, detail by detail.

That was just Edna June's way.

"This doesn't make sense," Jim said yet again, and then, leaving Mr. Thurman Sr. where he stood, he braced himself, gave Thurman Jr. a quick look, and the two of them walked purposely over to the Toyota FJ Cruiser to see what they could see.

All three men standing around the vehicle looked up with surprised irritation at the intrusion.

Jim looked to Police Chief Goody, Dr. Dennison (a smallish young man of twenty-seven in a gray tweed sports coat with a neatly-trimmed beard and moustache), and Mayor Elliott (dapper as always in a Hawaiian shirt, khaki slacks and tennis shoes without socks, exactly what Jim was wearing).

"This is total horseshit," Jim Starke said, sticking his nose right in.

Police Chief Orville Goody was the first to react.

"Gentlemen, this is an official investigation you're disrupting," he informed them. "You're behind the barricades out of courtesy to Mr. Thurman. I want you both to return to that area right now."

Jim ignored him.

"Good outfit, Mr. Mayor," Jim said, to which George Elliot nodded agreement with a slight smile. "We must have the same tailor."

Turning back to Police Chief Goody, he said, "We're here to identify the body."

He gestured back towards the elder Mr. Thurman, watching at a distance, yet clearly unwilling to come any nearer.

"Mr. Thurman doesn't need to see this."

Mayor Elliot, noticing Horace Thurman Sr. standing back in the woods for the first time, made a sympathetic gesture towards the man and nodded 'Hello.' He was a long-time friend of the Thurman family and, by extension, also a surprisingly good friend of Jim Starke.

He certainly felt their loss.

Police Chief Orville Goody took a deep breath, then let it out slowly. He was suddenly fuming at what he perceived to be a show of complete disrespect on Jim's part.

Dr. Dennison, with an effort carefully opened the rear driver's side door to the burned-out vehicle using a rubber-gloved hand, ignoring them all. He stepped back quickly as a river of black ash-filled water poured out the door and onto his heavy brown wingtips.

"Damn!"

The smell of burnt flesh, plastic and upholstery was almost overpowering, but the doctor seemed not to notice.

Mayor George Elliot said nothing, but watched warily, in case his authority to intervene between the police chief and the bereaved family would be called upon. It definitely wouldn't be the first time, not with a notoriously volatile lawman such as Orville Goody involved.

The man just had no finesse.

"We'll *inform* you when you can I.D. the body," the police chief announced to Jim and Thurman Jr. "It's not something you just decide for yourself. Until then, this is an investigation and you are not part of it. So I'm telling you, for the last time, go back over to where Mr. Thurman's standing *right now*!"

And, with the full authority of the law behind him, the large overbearing man said it so clearly, and with such threat and forcefulness, that he appeared truly amazed when Jim Starke merely stood before him, without flinching and without moving, as if merely waiting to see what the police chief might do next.

And the police chief, as if suddenly realizing Mayor Elliot and Dr. Dennison were both watching and wondering the same thing themselves, had to then take a quick second to decide exactly what that might be.

At that same moment, the rest of the forensic team from the county, one photographer, arrived to assist Dr. Dennison. A slight man in shirt-sleeves and tie, he was lugging his equipment through the woods and down the path that the Toyota FJ Cruiser had actually plowed straight into the tree.

The police chief, glancing up at the photographer's approach, used his arrival to partially defuse what he immediately saw as a probable tense confrontation with a member (pretty much) of the poor bereaved family, which could never play well anywhere, forget that that Thurman Jr. individual was an extremely dangerous man anyway, as likely to just go off as not.

Having to shoot the crazy fucker in front of the Mayor, and probable media people, would not be good.

"Hold on!" Police Chief Goody held out a big hand to the photographer. "You wait right there and we'll let you know when it's okay."

"What are you talking about, Chief?" the man stopped. "I'm just shooting the accident like always—"

Police Chief Orville Goody suddenly pointed at him with a thick finger.

"I'm telling you to wait and that means *wait!*" Orville Goody exploded. "Goddamn it, are you deaf?"

The photographer took a step back quickly, then waved it off. He'd obviously stand around all day, and tomorrow too, if that's what the police chief wanted.

"No problem."

"Now, as for *you*. . ." the Chief turned back to Jim Starke, but by then the Mayor was talking to Jim, quietly to the side.

A moment later, Mayor Elliot looked up and said to Police Chief Goody, "Orville, I think under the circumstances, it might be appropriate to let these boys here take a look, just for identification purposes, to spare poor Horace Thurman Sr. that tragic duty later in the day. I personally don't see the harm."

Jim stood by.

If it was true that Police Chief Goody hated him before, and hated the Thurman family just as fiercely, this certainly wasn't going to make the top lawman in Interception City any friendlier in the future.

The police chief took another breath, finally nodded tightly.

"Thank you, Orville," said the Mayor. "I'll remember it."

Without another word, Orville Goody turned and walked back over to the burned out vehicle to join Dr. Dennison.

It *was* true that Police Chief Orville Goody was a powerful and often frightening character for anyone to deal with in I.C., but anyone who knew anything about Banyon County or Interception City politics understood that the real power, the old boy network power, lay with George Elliott.

"Thanks, Mayor," Jim said. "As always."

Chapter 25

The blackened hulk of the Toyota FJ Cruiser, no longer smoldering but still smelling strongly of smoke and death, and finally, mostly, drained of water, stood against the huge scorched cypress tree as if permanently joining it.

It was not the first vehicle that ended its existence against that particular tree.

At Jim's and Thurman Jr.'s approach, Dr. Dennison stepped back out of the way as did, a long moment later, Police Chief Goody.

Through the open driver's side door, Jim could see the two charred bodies within, the as-yet-unidentified male behind the wheel, sitting stiffly (and oddly) at attention, his features, facial and otherwise, so melted beyond recognition it was impossible to say what race or age he'd been.

He hadn't skin any longer, regardless of what color it *had* been.

His mouth, open in an expression of fear or surprise, showed good strong teeth still intact, except for a narrow jagged hole where a front tooth had clearly and cleanly been knocked out.

Jim, looking, couldn't see what the man's mouth had hit, since he was sitting straight up and he was much taller than the steering wheel, but it seemed unlikely he'd gotten into the vehicle in that condition.

He leaned in slightly, careful to not touch anything, then tensed at the sight of Edna June Thurman's charred remains.

Poor burned Edna June lay partially over the console where she'd ended up, facing the driver but definitely without her face in his lap, as Orville Goody had specifically stated. It'd take a lot of imagination to come up with *that* scenario, although (and he admitted to himself it *was* possible, on further reflection) Jim could see that that *might* be the truth here as well.

Luckily, Jim could only see the back of Edna June's head, hair melted to her blackened scalp, her body charred and burned nude, yet with an occasional scrap of ash-like clothing adhering to her flesh.

That he had been with her only the afternoon before—and now here she was, a blackened shell all that remained of the woman—both astonished and grieved him greatly.

He didn't want to see her face.

"Recognize that…?" Thurman Jr. pointed.

On her left wrist, Jim immediately recognized the expensive silver watch and band, blackened thoroughly, that he and Thurman Jr. (over twenty years earlier) had chipped in to buy for her birthday. She had never stopped wearing that watch and seeing it made Jim tighten up inside.

"Yeah."

His eyes were suddenly moist.

He let out a breath, then they walked around the vehicle to see what the situation looked like from the other side.

"We can't let the press in here," the Mayor was saying, by the open passenger door, and the others were definitely listening. "Or even our own forensic photographer. Not yet. I don't want Edna June remembered this way."

"I agree," the police chief said. "Let's get the two of 'em out of there, toss that dead coon in the trash heap, and forget his ass completely."

Which caused both Mayor Elliot and Dr. Dennison to simply stare at him, clearly shocked.

"What?" Orville Goody went on. "We write him up as a John Doe DOA. Hell, we found his charred black ass hanging in an orange grove, the way I remember it. Makes it all real clear..."

There was a long silence.

Finally, Mayor Elliot said, "Orville, that's a hell of a plan, but I'm not certain that's what we need to do. It's just a little too. . .too. . ."

"...too Ku Klux Klan," Jim finished the thought.

Dr. Dennison coughed nervously, kept his eyes to the ground. He obviously knew the way things worked in the real world, or at least in Banyon County, and that the decision here would not, ultimately, be his, regardless of the way it was *supposed* to be done.

Police Chief Orville Goody fixed Jim Starke with a look of pure hatred.

He was *not* afraid of Jim Starke, or his crazy fucking sidekick Thurman Jr., either, even though half the goddamn city always got real jumpy when either of those boys' names were mentioned.

Orville Goody had no idea why.

He had the full force of the law behind him, after all, and he wanted Jim and Thurman Jr. to understand exactly that. Orville Goody was the rightful Police Chief of Interception City, goddamn it, and the community was supposed to fear *him*, not the other way around.

Jim Starke met the man's hard glare and held it.

"I have no fight with you, Chief," he finally said, easily. "I'm looking for the truth, too, so I'd say we're on the same side."

And Mayor Elliott, who understood timing if nothing else, seized the moment, jumping right in on that note of positive cooperation.

"We *are* on the same side," he said. "So let's act like it."

He then gestured expansively for calm, enough of this petty bickering among men with a common goal in mind, and asked them each to consider how the awkwardness of the matter before them might be resolved.

Throughout it all, Thurman Jr. stood by stoically, saying nothing. His presence, however, was very much noted—by all of them.

"I don't believe it's necessary," the mayor continued, clearly considering the *sensitivity* of his mostly redneck constituency, "to mention the, uh, race of the gentleman who'd gone, uh, riding with Edna June last night." And with a glance into the vehicle, he suddenly realized, and asked, "Who's to say for certain that he was, in fact, black?"

And with that, Jim Starke saw the chance he'd waited for.

"Chief Goody, why *did* you tell Mr. Thurman the man was black? How could you tell, with him burnt-up like that?"

And the police chief, clearly caught off-guard by the question, seemed to think about it for a very long moment without answering. The others looked to him, too, perhaps suddenly wondering the same thing.

They had all just assumed, after all. . .

"He's black," the police chief suddenly insisted, pointing. "Damn it all to hell, look at the bastard! He's a black damn bastard, as any idiot can see!"

The others looked, but clearly did not see.

"He's black *now*," Jim agreed. "But a white man would be, too."

He turned to Dr. Dennison, the Banyon County Coroner and obviously the single person standing there most likely, most qualified in every way, to know the truth of the matter.

"Doctor, *is* it a black man?"

And Dr. Dennison froze and, plainly enough for anyone with half or more of a brain to see: *pretended* to take a real good look across at the charred corpse behind the steering wheel, nodding as he did so, as if he hadn't just spent every moment since he'd arrived looking at the damn thing, the learned man suddenly appearing to study the driver's remains with every ounce of his professional know-how and stalling, stalling, stalling.

Goddamn this pushy redneck cracker Jim Starke, the good doctor had to be thinking.

It was obvious that in no way did he want to contradict Police Chief Orville Goody, a terrifying man who knew how to make good on a threat or carry out a grudge in return for embarrassing him in public in any way whatsoever. The police chief's mean-spirited eyes were already boring into the side of the man's face, daring the young doctor to say anything other than that the dead driver was the blackest goddamn bastard son of a bitch that ever lived.

Period!

"Well, absolutely, yes, the man might be black," Dr. Dennison started, and coughed again, but it only postponed the inevitable, an expansion on his qualified answer to them all, which he couldn't really avoid. "On the other hand, it's very difficult to say with any certainty that the man is, in fact, an African-American, in his current state. Of course, after certain laboratory tests. . ."

Jim continued to pinion the man with a look.

"You can't tell, can you?" he asked, and Dr. Dennison looked away, clearly needing to be far, far away, and didn't answer. Jim turned back to the police chief, and looking at him straight on as well, asked again, "So, Chief Goody, how did *you* know he was black?"

And waited.

If there had been no witnesses present, Jim Starke was certain Police Chief Orville Goody would have yanked out his chrome-plated .357 Magnum and shot him dead right where he stood.

That this. . .*friend* of the family, not even a real relative of the Thurman's, would put him on the spot in front of the others, asking questions as if he was interrogating the police chief himself, drove the very large man almost insane with anger.

"Goddamn it!" Orville Goody finally sputtered, resting his wide hand on the solid butt of his heavy revolver as if to emphasize the serious turn the conversation had taken. "I don't have to answer your damn questions! You're supposed to answer mine—"

Jim said simply, "Mr. Mayor. . ."

And the police chief, cornered, and knowing he hadn't answered the question but realizing he eventually would have to, said, "Officer John Pasco told me it was a damn nigger when he called this morning. How the hell do I know what race the burned-up son of a bitch is, if the fucking Coroner—" and here he glared at Dr. Dennison, who flinched "—can't even tell?"

Which was the exact moment Walter Hightower stepped into the clearing, just in time to hear the I.C. lawman's racist description of the dead man.

Chapter 26

"Who the hell are you?" Police Chief Goody asked.

Walter stared at the blackened hulk of Edna June's Toyota FJ Cruiser, then opened his sport coat wider to reveal his .44 Magnum and badge. He'd overheard the local lawman's casual use of the big 'N' word and, although not surprised by it, he was nonetheless annoyed to say the least.

These cracker *bastards*.

"I'm Officer Walter Hightower, Florida Department of Law Enforcement," he said, with authority. "I'm looking for an undercover FDLE officer who disappeared in this vicinity last night." And here he fixed Police Chief Orville Goody with a particularly baleful look. "A black officer, driving a black Corvette sports car."

And the police chief, possibly reacting but clearly trying not to show it, turned away just as another redneck officer of the law, a skinny peckerwood all in black like he was going to a Halloween party, walked up to them all.

"Sorry," Orville Goody, turning back, finally said to Walter. "Doesn't ring a bell." And to this new peckerwood, he asked, "Officer Lanyard, we seen a black man in a black Corvette sports car in the vicinity…?"

The skinny Officer Lanyard was quick to answer.

"No sir, Chief. Not a black man in a black Corvette sports car. That's a combination I'd surely remember."

"This man, this *officer*," Chief Goody pointed out, meaning Walter, "is from FDLE, says their missing man is with their department…another black man from the Florida Department of Law Enforcement himself. We know anything about that, Ray?"

And Officer Ray Lanyard swallowed hard, then turned his eyes away before answering.

"No, sir, we sure don't."

Chief Goody shook his head with what appeared to be actual disgust, then put on a smile for *Officer* Walter Hightower and gestured, "Got us an SUV right here, dead man of an unidentified race burned up to a black cinder behind the wheel…"

Walter stiffened.

Chief Goody then gestured to Thurman Jr. as he added, "Burned up man was next to this gentleman's mother in the vehicle, an influential white woman, got herself killed in a somewhat unsavory manner—"

To which Thurman Jr. finally began to react, but was stopped by a quick look from Jim Starke, an action which Walter Hightower very much noticed.

He stared at the two extremely dangerous-looking rednecks, both of them every black man's worst down-South nightmare. Then he just shook his head. Neither of them reacted to his look.

Exhaling slowly, Walter steeled himself, moved to the burned-out SUV and looked inside. What he saw confirmed his worst fear: that *had* to be Elmore in there, but he was unwilling to let these racist bastards see his pain.

He stepped back.

"Chief, as of this moment this entire investigation will be handled by FDLE. Have your men secure the perimeter, then stay back until our crew gets here."

Orville Goody reacted as expected.

"Now, hold on, son..."

Walter Hightower ignored the heavy-set police chief, got out his cell phone, woke up Lt. Scribner.

"Lieutenant, we got a real problem here in a skid-mark called Interception City, need the forensics crew from Miami." He listened. Then, "Yeah, it's Elmore."

Jim and Thurman Jr. exchanged a look. The dead man really *was* a black FDLE officer burned up in the SUV?!

Giving Jim Starke and Thurman Jr. a harsh look, Walter went on, "It's yokel redneck central, looks like they didn't appreciate an educated black man spending time with one of their fancy white trash women…"

Neither Jim nor Thurman Jr. reacted, instead merely met his gaze.

Police Chief Orville Goody, immediately seeing the implications, and the advantage to himself and Officer Ray, exhaled and then motioned for Ray Lanyard and Dr. David Dennison to follow as he simply turned and walked out of the woods.

Mayor George Elliot clapped Jim Starke on the shoulder with a look after Chief Goody's back.

"Jim-boy, I'd stay out of that big man's way for a while."

"Mr. Mayor, I'm not sure I can do that."

Which got a shake of the head from the mayor before he excused himself to Officer Hightower, then walked out to talk to Mr. Thurman Sr., his old friend.

Walter fixed Jim and Thurman Jr. with a look that was anything but friendly. Or in any way tolerant.

"You-all can move on the fuck out of here, too."

Jim calmly said, "So the man *is* black—"

Walter stared at him for a long moment..

"Boy…"

"We're not your problem," Jim told him.

But Walter Hightower wasn't hearing it. He stepped closer, opened his coat again to emphasize who was in charge here.

"Move your goddamn cracker asses out of here now, boy. I'm the goddamn law."

"Yessir, Officer Watermelon," Thurman Jr. said.

"Jesus Christ, Thurman—"

Thurman Jr., ready for a showdown anytime, anywhere, said, "He wants to play that fucking game, let's go!"

And Walter and Thurman Jr. squared off, Jim realizing it'd be hard to say which one would live through the encounter. Finally, moving between them, he managed to move Thurman Jr. away.

As Walter watched, the two rednecks he'd just met headed back to the road.

He turned back to the Toyota FJ Cruiser, couldn't believe his older brother was dead in there. Getting out his cell phone again, he hit a speed dial button, his eyes tearing up while it rang on the other end.

"Mom...?" he said when she answered.

Chapter 27

The first thing Jim Starke and Thurman Jr. saw when they walked out of the woods was Wendy Jamison-Johnson standing with Mr. Thurman Sr., both of them next to a slate gray Lincoln that had been pulled over onto the shoulder.

It'd apparently been allowed into the barricaded area and was wedged in, nose-first, between Jim's red CJ-5 and Mr. Thurman's Buick Park Avenue.

As they reached them, Wendy turned to Thurman Jr., stepped up and actually startled him with a quick hug.

"Thurman, it's so awful about your mother," she said. "I just can't believe it."

"Thanks. I don't believe it, either."

She turned to Jim then and he felt everything within him suddenly melt. Especially when she leaned into him, kissed his cheek lightly but then just as suddenly surprised him with an impulsive quick kiss on the lips.

Their first kiss ever, in fact. He'd never even come close to kissing her in the past. But it told Jim Starke there was definitely something there. Or at least that there *could* be.

"Hello, Jim," she said then. "It's been a long time."

"Wendy. It has. You're back, huh?"

He was obviously still something of an idiot when it came to Wendy.

Her exceptionally blue eyes met his for a long moment, holding the gaze, and it was Jim, finally, who blinked and looked away. And even though twenty years had passed, to him she looked exactly the same as the day she'd left.

She was in loose-fitting jeans and a simple unadorned white tee shirt, her short blonde hair casually brushed back and up in a boyish way that somehow made her seem fifteen again, her delicate, perfectly formed ears accented with small, plain gold earrings. Her lipstick was pale pink, almost unnoticeable really, and she otherwise appeared to be wearing no makeup at all, her skin entirely fresh and astonishingly young-looking.

"It's so awful about poor Mrs. Thurman," Wendy said.

"Did Edna June know you were coming back?"

Which got a surprised look from both of the Thurman's, Jr. and Sr., but they said nothing.

Wendy seemed surprised at the question also, but she nodded and said, "I talked to her on the phone just yesterday morning, expecting to see her at the reunion. Actually, to see *all* of you."

Thurman Jr. had to laugh at that.

"Jim and I weren't invited," he told her. "We didn't graduate, remember? We both got kicked out that last year."

Jim shook his head at her sudden look.

"Guess you forgot that, huh?"

"I don't believe this," Wendy said. "I *did* forget all about that. Now I'm not sure I want to go either…"

But Thurman Jr. gave her a look.

"Hey, you graduated," he said. "Don't miss the damn reunion on our account."

She was silent for a long moment.

"Well. . ." she was still undecided. "I *am* curious about it, I'll admit. Maybe I'll just drop in…"

"You can tell us who's still a loser and who's become one," Jim said.

He knew his I.C. classmates only too well.

"Maybe you could come as my guests," she then suggested.

Jim Starke and Thurman Jr. exchanged a glance.

"Yeah, what the hell," Jim said. "If everybody's there, maybe we can get an idea of what really happened out here…"

Meaning the burned-out SUV with Edna June and the black FDLE officer. A notion which immediately shocked Wendy. And Mr. Thurman himself, who apparently hadn't considered such a notion.

"You don't think it's an accident...?" Wendy asked.

"I don't think anything," Jim admitted. "Yet."

Jennifer finally sat up in Wendy's Lincoln.

Mr. Thurman Sr. noticed and asked Wendy, "Is that your daughter?"

All of them turned to see the teen girl, sitting up finally in the passenger seat where she'd been trying to get back to sleep. She pointedly turned her face away and stared out the other side rather than acknowledge her mother's old I.C. friends.

"She's not happy to be here," Wendy admitted. "I'm not so sure I should have brought her, after all, but Judge Leonard Johnson and I are going through a bad divorce and I thought it might do her good to get away."

She looked back into the car, where Jennifer continued to ignore them.

"Maybe not."

While they talked, Jim noticed Walter Hightower had moved up to the edge of the road and was writing down their license plate numbers.

"That FDLE cop..." Thurman Jr. said, then waved with a smile and nodded to the man, who gave him back an extremely hostile look before again ignoring them all. "I think he's going to be a problem."

Wendy turned to the Lincoln, opened the passenger side door.

"Jennifer," Wendy said, a little sharply. "Please be polite. I want you to meet three good friends of mine.

And the young girl finally exhaled loudly, theatrically, and turned to face them without moving from her seat.

"I'm pleased to meet you," Jennifer said. *Not.*

"Out of the car, please."

"God. . ." the girl shook her head.

Chapter 28

Orlando

At the exact moment Wendy Jamison-Johnson was introducing her daughter on the shoulder of County Road 823 to Jim Starke, Horace Thurman Jr. and Mr. Thurman Sr., Federal Judge Leonard Johnson (currently on judicial suspension) knelt before the bulky black safe in the back of his closet, the closet situated in his house.

Actually, it was in the large house that only Wendy and their daughter Jennifer currently occupied, by court order.

He stayed away from the windows, not wanting a nosy neighbor seeing him and contacting the police, believing it to be a burglar or even, in fact, the judge himself. He had no idea who knew he wasn't supposed to be there and who didn't, but he was taking no chances.

As soon as Wendy and Jennifer had driven away early that morning, in the dark, neither looking back to the garage door as it automatically closed, he'd dashed in from his hiding place lying under the oleanders alongside the garage and literally rolled under the heavy metal door just before it met the concrete floor.

He'd stood then, brushed himself off, and went directly to the glass jar half-filled with old nails and screws on the shelf over the workbench, *his* workbench, damn that ex-wife of his to hell. He dumped the contents of the jar onto the workbench, quickly got out his extra house-key, then put the pile of nails and screws back into the jar. He put the jar back on the shelf.

It was important Wendy not know he had returned, nor that he *could* return, whenever he felt like it, thanks to the hidden key he'd long kept from her.

He shook his head with a smug smile at the thought.

Unlocking and opening the solid door leading from the garage into the kitchen had presented another serious problem, the alarm immediately buzzing its forty-five second warning, waiting for the code.

Leonard was enormously pleased to discover, however, that he *was* as brilliant as he'd always assumed himself to be: after first punching in the old four-digit code, his birthday, he immediately tried Wendy's birthday (too many digits, actually, five), and then cleared it and tried Jennifer's birthday, four-digits like his own, and the buzzing stopped.

Not only did he have a key, he told himself proudly, he now also knew the new alarm code.

He'd always thought his wife was exceptionally bright but, apparently, she was no match for Judge Leonard Johnson himself.

To give himself plenty of time, and to assure no other housebreaker interrupted or surprised him in the middle of his own housebreaking, he cleverly reset the alarm to INSTANT using the code he'd discovered.

That would give him an immediate warning if anyone else, for whatever reason, unexpectedly showed up.

He then spent the next two hours searching the house, *his* house still, damn it, familiarizing himself with the changes his absence had brought about, before getting to the real business at hand, the safe.

In the three weeks since he'd been banished, little had changed, actually, but he noticed many more feminine items lying around in the two women's bathrooms (shampoos and conditioners and hair dryers and curlers and many things he couldn't identify), not put away as he'd always demanded.

Just as he'd always believed: with no man around to make them keep those small rooms neat, they quickly became pigsties.

In Wendy's bedroom, on her desk, he discovered her open calendar showing a 10:00 A.M. Monday meeting with the Florida State Attorney up in Tallahassee concerning the disappearance of the entire account for her *Psychic Trailer Park Hotline* cable TV show.

He couldn't find any correspondence or notes regarding any actual conversations she'd had with that particular office, but he was certain his name had been prominent throughout any talks they'd had.

She'd definitely blame Leonard for that particular criminal act.

Of course, he *did* have the money he'd emptied from the account (with help from a very nice embezzler from Miami he'd met professionally two years earlier), most of it stashed away in a safe place, over forty thousand dollars less ten percent to his helpful embezzler associate. He would gladly give back what was left of that money without a qualm, he thought, but there were now actual criminal charges forthcoming to be dealt with.

The sudden thought of prison, certain death for an ex-judge, of course, chilled him to the bone.

On her calendar also, scribbled hastily into today's date, was a single phone number with 'I.C.' next to it, in an area code Leonard knew to be Banyon County. He started to pick up the phone on Wendy's desk, than hesitated a moment.

Instead, he first stepped into her bathroom and rooted around through her clothes hamper.

He came out of the bathroom door a few minutes later with a tiny pair of Wendy's cotton panties in his hand. Through her panties (light blue with a small navy bunny at the hip), he punched in the phone number.

"I.C. Motel," a female voice announced.

"The I.C. Motel in Interception City?"

"Where else, you numbskull...?"

He hung up without another word. He then studied the panties in his hand, finally put them into his pocket.

* * *

He knew the heavy safe in their bedroom closet held the corporate checkbooks, payroll journals and deposit records. These were the items, the 'books' as it were, that needed to disappear and to disappear fast.

As a judge, he'd seen more than one criminal case evaporate when the paper evidence had disappeared in smoke, and only innuendo and supposition, with no physical proof, was left to support the prosecution's vague theories.

The only other problem, then, would be Wendy herself testifying against him and that might or might not occur.

Many non-lawyers believed a wife could not testify against a husband in a court of law, but that was not the case. Rather, a wife could not be *made* to testify against her husband, a very big difference: Wendy would certainly volunteer to testify, if it came to that, for reasons of spite or self-preservation.

That was a big problem, a terrifyingly big problem, in fact, but he would have to deal with it later.

Leonard used Wendy's blue panties to dial the safe combination (which had always been his birthday), but was not at all surprised when it failed. He then dialed in Jennifer's birthday and (what an idiot that woman was!), the last click told him the safe was open.

With a smile, he pushed down the heavy handle, then pulled open the solid door, feeling it snag on something for a moment and so he pulled harder—only to be instantly blinded and nearly choked to death by the pepper spray/capistan canister which suddenly went off.

It was the only thing within.

It had been duct-taped to the inside of the safe, pointing outward, a wire with only minimum slack attached across the trigger on top, the other end duct-taped to the inside of the heavy door. When the wire pulled the trigger as the door opened, the canister emptied a serious blast of its fiery contents directly into Leonard's wide-open expectant face in a scant half-second.

He literally screamed.

"*That bitch!*" he gasped, unable to breathe, his eyes so instantly swollen and stinging and filled with tears he literally could not open them, his nose overflowing with more than enough mucus to match.

He was a sudden river of disgusting fluids.

He barely managed to stand, so overcome was he by the astonishingly acrid fumes, even after he'd managed somehow to close the safe. Blindly making his way into the hallway, he could concentrate only on trying to get away, as far away as possible, from those killing fumes.

By the time he'd found his way into the kitchen, crying out as well as moaning from his very real pain, he feared he might be permanently blind, so great was the burning agony, and he frantically pushed his face under the faucet and turned on the cold water, full blast, holding his face there but *still* unable to open his eyes and so merely half-drowning himself in the attempt.

"Son of a bitch!" he panted.

He jerked away from the sink and searched for a dish towel, a dishcloth, even a paper towel, a paper bag, any damn thing to wipe his horribly stinging eyes (unable, actually, to recall where *anything* in the goddamn kitchen was!), then suddenly remembered Wendy's light blue panties in his pocket, which, even blind, he was able to find.

With the pair of his soon-to-be-ex-wife's underpants to his face, wiping furiously and *still* unable to open his eyes, he yanked open the first door he came to, the one leading into the garage, and even in his insane pain heard the piercing burglar alarm instantly go off.

It shattered the air with its insistent call to the police, the neighbors, and anyone else within earshot.

"Jesus Christ!"

Panicking finally, Federal Judge Leonard Johnson tried near-hysterically to find the alarm keypad on the wall, which he managed to do quickly, but was then unable to punch in the actual code, for there were many odd symbols which made up the set and several were located before the real numbers started.

"God *damn* it!"

Trying desperately to remember the lay-out of the keypad, but failing again and again, he repeatedly and doggedly punched in the numerical equivalent of Jennifer's birthday, the screeching alarm continuing to wail, until finally he heard a different sound, police car sirens, heading straight for him.

If Leonard had been panicked before, he was now on the verge of an actual stroke, so terrified was he of being caught.

He was definitely breaking the law, breaking into his ex-wife's house, and he knew it, and the police would instantly know it, having a computer record of his restraining order at their fingertips in the squad car. That, coupled with Wendy's Monday morning meeting with the State Attorney's office (where any Investigator alive would instantly understand what he was in the house searching for), would be the end of him.

He did the only thing he could think of.

He ran.

First blindly groping around and finding the garage-door button on the inside garage wall keypad, he pushed it. Then, listening for the automatic door to take forever to open, and timing it perfectly, he finally ran like hell straight out of the garage through the open door, down the driveway and into the tall bushes off to the side, where he would hide out and wait for his eyes to finally open so he could sneak away while the cops searched the house.

At least, that was his plan.

Unfortunately, the garage-door-button he pushed was the one that opened the *second* garage door where his Lincoln used to sit, *not* the door he'd entered through. After waiting so impatiently he thought he might actually wet himself, the big metal garage door he thought was wide open was so solidly in place he actually made a giant clanging *KA-WHAM!!!* sound when he ran full-force into it, nearly knocking himself out and landing flat on his back on the cement garage floor.

In fact, the sound was so loud, even above the screeching alarm, it instantly alerted the two police officers in the squad car pulling up into the driveway.

"What the fuck. . ?!"

The two officers glanced at each other with clear apprehension, then immediately yanked out their guns.

"I'm Federal Judge Leonard Johnson," Leonard announced from his back on the floor, trying to be heard through the closed garage door, but now crying hysterically. "Help me, I'm blind!"

Wendy's tiny blue cotton panties were still held to his eyes, tears and mucus streaming unabated, when he heard the two big cops suddenly charge into the garage through the other (open) garage door, guns drawn and expecting *anything*.

"I'm a federal judge!" Leonard continued to wail.

But through the tears, panties and mucus, it came out: "I'm a febril jlugb!"

The two cops slammed to a halt, covering Leonard with both weapons, just in case he tried anything.

God only knew what the hell kind of sicko deal they had here, it looking like a young girl's underpants the deranged bastard was still sniffing and rubbing into his eyes, unwilling to stop, even with the cops standing right in his face with the drop on the crazy son of a bitch.

"It's gotta be angel-dust..." the older cop announced.

The younger cop, suddenly putting it all together in his head, the open door to the house, the screaming alarm still, the tiny panties, this lunatic squirming around on the ground, suddenly realized:

"Jesus, I'll bet this doped-up bastard just raped or killed the people live here, a little girl, too, it looks like from those underpants!"

His face turned bright red, his finger tightening on the trigger, his expression almost as crazed as the bastard squirming on the floor.

"I oughta blow this sick-fuck's brains out—"

And for a very real moment, it sounded to Leonard (who then *did* wet himself) like the young cop was actually going to do it.

"I'm a goddamn jlugb!" Leonard wailed again, but it at least stopped the young cop from pulling the trigger while he tried to understand just what in the hell this psychopath was trying to say.

In case it was a confession.

The older, more mature cop, as unnerved as his partner by the sight before them, yet trying to maintain calm, suggested to the younger man:

"We'd better call this in!"

Chapter 29

In the backseat of the squad car, hands cuffed in front of him instead of behind him as a concession to the overreaction by the two Orlando P.D. officers who'd first arrived at the scene, Federal Judge Leonard Johnson was finally regaining his composure and able to think about something, anything, other than his burning eyes, which finally seemed much better.

He'd managed, when back-up in the form of four screeching police cars showed up to further subdue him, in the confusion to drop the pair of Wendy's stolen panties he was clutching into the bushes alongside the driveway, unnoticed while everyone was yelling at everyone else.

That he really *was* a federal judge (suspended or not) had vaguely unsettled the higher ranking officers, who better knew just who the hell they were fucking with here, not a good idea at all.

However, Leonard *had* broken the law, more than one law, in fact, and would have to be taken downtown and booked, forget that he'd simply post bail and be out in less than two minutes.

It was still official procedure and had to be followed.

His worry, oddly enough, now that he could think a bit clearer, was his ex-wife's *second* pair of panties, lacy sheer white, which he'd stolen from the hamper along with the first, his idea of a spare, still safely in his *other* front pants pocket where he'd stuffed them.

They'd easily been missed during the pat-down.

But he knew that during his booking the attendant would more thoroughly search him, pockets inside out, and the woman's underwear would be found, and then written into the booking report as such.

Brought in directly from the break-in of his ex-wife's house, it would be more than evident to anyone that the soiled panties were his ex-wife's and he would forever be branded a pathetic weirdo.

A label he'd couldn't stand.

White-collar crime was one thing, and even burglary had its flair, but stealing his ex-wife's panties was something else entirely!

Much worse, actually. Far more embarrassing.

When the police car exited at 33rd Street, it was clear he would have to act quickly, the new downtown lock-up less than two minutes away, so with his fingertips (and carefully watching the two cops in the front seat) he managed to reach into his front pocket and snag Wendy's panties.

He slowly pulled them out, compressed them into a tiny ball, then leaned far forward and violently coughed (a little cover move there), at the same time popping them into his mouth.

It was his plan—based on many actual cases where drug smugglers had ingested condoms and many other odd articles filled with illegal substances—to simply swallow Wendy's underpants.

When he sat back up, the shotgun cop, another younger one, was looking at him oddly.

"Sir, you okay back there?"

"Um hum," Leonard nodded, then quickly turned his head to look out the side window as if he'd never seen downtown Orlando before, where his own office had been located for over seventeen years.

The shotgun cop finally turned around to continue talking to his partner, but a moment later turned *back* around at the muffled choking noises Leonard was making, the judge's handcuffed hands to his face as he tried desperately, with his fingers, to claw *something* out of his throat.

"Jesus, Stan!" the driver said, looking into the rearview mirror. "He's choking back there!"

Already on the radio, the shotgun cop immediately called in, "Need emergency assistance, 911 paramedics for choking prisoner! We're taking him to O.R.M.C., meet us at Emergency!"

"Christ, he's turning blue!" the driver said, hitting the brakes hard and stopping dead in the middle of traffic, sideways. "Get back there and save his ass! They'll kill us, we lose a fucking judge in the backseat!"

"What the fuck's he got in his mouth?!"

But the shotgun cop was already out the door even as he said it, pulling open the back door and hauling the handcuffed Leonard out onto the street so fast he almost gave the choking judge whiplash.

Wrapping his arms around Leonard from behind in the classic Heimlich Maneuver, he squeezed hard, but nothing happened.

He did it again, harder, almost breaking the man's ribs the second time, but whatever the object was, it would not dislodge.

The young cop then pushed Leonard down flat on his back, straddled him suddenly, right in the middle of stopped traffic in all directions. While many of the drivers got out to see what was going on, the young cop held Leonard's flailing handcuffed hands down out of the way and literally forced his fingers down into the judge's throat at the same time.

"What *is* it. . ?!" the cop trying to save him wanted to know, at last hooking a finger into whatever it was and pulling hard.

Leonard, rapidly losing consciousness, finally felt Wendy's white underpants dislodge from his windpipe, his sudden inhalation of breath so unexpected and sweet, he suddenly burst into tears again.

The officer who'd been driving, impatiently motioning for downtown traffic to get back into your fucking cars and go around, you goddamn blockheads (fucking Orlando tourists were all idiots!), watched as his partner administered what he guessed could be considered First Aid to a possibly dying man right in the middle of the street.

The driver cop was amazed a quick moment later to see a crumpled white pair of girl's panties suddenly pulled from Federal Judge Leonard Johnson's throat, his partner dangling them on his fingertip and holding them up for the entire crowd of onlookers to see.

"Panties," the younger cop announced, standing then, to a round of sincere but confused applause. "Another pair of goddamn panties!"

"What's *with* this guy. . ?!" the driver cop wondered aloud.

And Leonard, slowly regaining his senses for the second time that same morning, and gradually becoming aware of the throng of curious spectators who had witnessed the fiasco (including a cameraman from Channel 9!), and with a pretty good idea of the notations that would be entered onto his booking report, sat up and (his will to live going fast) seriously considered just running in front of the next Lynx bus that happened by.

The only thing, then, that enabled him to finally get to his feet, to get right up in front of the entire world and climb back into the backseat of the squad car, which would then take him to jail, were thoughts of revenge.

Justice and revenge, actually, as he saw it, every fiber of his being concentrating, suddenly, on the solitary person whose lack of understanding and compassion had started this entire hellish mess in the first place (and thus, effectively ended the judge's very good life): Wendy Jamison-Johnson.

The judge at last knew what his next move would be, *after* he retrieved the '*Psychic Trailer Park Hotline*' books.

Keen deduction on his part, having searched the house thoroughly, told him she was keeping the books with her, so it was his next-to-the-next move really, and that would be, simply, to have the inconsiderate bitch killed.

It would involve a quick cellphone call to his embezzler cohort in Miami as soon as he had a moment of privacy, but that should prove simple enough.

The main thing was, Wendy had to die.

Chapter 30

Interception City

Wendy pulled her big Lincoln up to the single hanging stoplight downtown and took a good look around.

In the early morning light, she could see that nothing much had changed in Interception City since she'd left all those years ago, the four sparse corners of the intersection of I.C. Boulevard and Old Sugar Lake Road still mainly what there was to the place.

"It's even worse than I thought," Jennifer saw fit to point out

And Wendy saw no point in arguing.

Downtown I.C. *was* awful after all, and she'd said it herself many times over the years. It was, apparently, exactly as she'd remembered it.

The I.C. Convenience Store owned by the Thurman family took up one corner, the two simple uncovered gas pumps she recalled still in front, the gray block building itself needing paint.

As always.

A large standing sign in front announced it was open for business 24-hours a day and that Florida Lotto tickets were sold there. A dilapidated pay phone booth stood off to one side, the phone book and the handset long gone.

Directly across from the store and facing it on the other side of I.C. Boulevard sat the combination Interception City Police Department and City Hall, the shared one-story red brick building on a small patch of sandy ground. A few drooping tropical trees and naturally-growing flowers set the place off from its drab surroundings.

A brown bud Allamanda vine, cut low and thick like a shrub, circled the paint-chipped gray flag pole in front, the vine's large bright yellow flowers highly striking but mostly poisonous to humans.

Wendy wondered if the city's maintenance person even realized it.

One police car sat behind the building, the other two and the Chief's vehicle apparently still out on CR 823 attending to Edna June's fatal accident.

On the third corner, a vacant lot since Wendy could remember, stood a permanent wooden For Sale sign, requesting interested parties call Horace Thurman Sr. at a local phone number.

"And look how decrapitated that huge house is!" Jennifer continued, one of her own favorite made-up words.

She was studying the monstrous Victorian-style home that occupied the entire fourth corner at a diagonal across from the I.C. Police Station.

"It's so creepy, like it's haunted!"

"That's the Thurman place."

The huge ramshackle home, two tall grim faded stories and three third-floor attic dormers, straight out of a fairy tale, or a nightmare, *did* look haunted.

It took up so much of the lot there was hardly any room for a lawn, and small patches of weed-like grass grew in what space there was. A rusted wire fence, low anyway and down in several spots, ran completely around the property and ended at two oddly thin but tall stone gateposts that no longer held gates.

The driveway, leading through the gateposts to an old one-car garage around the back, was simply sand and tufts of the same brown weed-like grass.

"It really is creepy," the teen said yet again.

From where she sat at the intersection, Wendy could also see, just over the trees, the stained and corroded silver-gray water tower behind the old high school in the distance, to the right of that the weathered spire, complete with modest cross, of the small I.C. Church of God she'd attended as a child.

More closely, glimpsed down each narrow side street branching away from the crossroads, were small dirty homes, many with corrugated tin roofs and unpainted solid plywood doors, and several poorly maintained house trailers in haphazard order, the dingy dwellings interspersed with ragged swampy overgrown fields.

It was not an inspiring sight.

Taking it all in for the first time in years, remembering it all at once, her entire young life at a glance almost, made Wendy suddenly feel like crying. She felt her eyes moisten and then, a moment later (surprising herself even more than Jennifer) she *was* crying.

And was unable to stop.

Quickly, she pulled over to the far side of the intersection and put the car into Park.

"Mom . . !" her daughter started, embarrassed at her mother's sudden display and clearly uncertain how to react. "Mother, damn it! Are you okay?"

Wendy put her forehead on the padded steering wheel, cried herself quickly out, well aware of how silly she must look to Jennifer. She hadn't allowed herself tears in years, and long ago thought it was no longer part of her nature, tough-minded business professional that she was.

It was just not something she did.

She finally got control of herself, dug tissue out of her purse, wiped her eyes and blew her nose. Without looking over at the girl, she said to her daughter, "Sorry about that. I guess I'm finally cracking up."

Jennifer said nothing, but when Wendy looked over to the girl, it was obvious that her teen daughter had tears in her eyes as well, although she did her best to hide the fact. Nothing could be worse than crying along with your own mom, except maybe letting your mom know it.

"Are you okay now?" Jennifer asked, back to her tough young self. Then, "What was *that* all about?"

Feeling better, Wendy put the car into Drive, pulled out and then made a right turn onto I.C. Boulevard, heading straight out to her folks' place.

"I don't even know," she said honestly. "I really don't. . ."

"I'll bet it's coming back to this terrible place after all these years."

And so, after three weeks of unrelieved anger and stoic resistance, Jennifer had apparently decided to resume talking to her mother, if only sparingly and still with a definite edge to her voice.

But at least they were talking.

"It's exactly that," Wendy agreed, "I remembered it as run-down and pretty much awful, but it's still a shock seeing it so. . . poor. It's like you said at home: white trash trailer park losers and I'm one of them."

"Mother. . ."

"It's true. Wait until you see where I grew up. You'll be shocked."

They rode in silence for a long moment.

"Is that where we're going now?"

"Yes."

"Is that where we're staying?" Jennifer wanted to know.

Wendy shook her head with a laugh and a quick look at the girl.

"I wouldn't do that to you. We're staying out at the I.C. Motel on the edge of town. But we need to meet my family today and I'd rather do it during daylight. I don't want an alligator running off with you in the dark—"

"Mom, you better be kidding!"

"You'll see. Anyway, I'll be watching out for you."

And her daughter actually laughed at that, the first time she'd laughed at *anything* in Wendy's presence since she'd learned of the impending divorce.

"Thank God, I have my mother to protect me."

"I might be a lot tougher than you think," Wendy told her.

"Were you a real tomboy growing up around here?"

Wendy thought about it.

"Not that I really noticed," she said. Then, "I guess so, but probably like any other girl living out in the country."

"What about those two guys we just met?" Jennifer wanted to know. "With the older man?"

"Mr. Thurman, you mean. We'll stop by to see him later tonight. He's an extremely nice gentleman. And I still can't believe his wife, Edna

June, is dead. I really wanted you to meet her, too."

That got a look from the girl suggesting nothing could interest her less, but she (nicely) kept her thoughts to herself.

"The two other guys were scary."

Wendy gave her a look.

"Did you really think so?"

"Don't *you* think so?" Jennifer seemed surprised. "My God, they're both just so...tough looking, like they should be in prison or something."

"They're not criminals." She thought about it. "Not really."

"The bigger one's got that terrible scar across his nose! And the other one, almost as tall with such cold eyes..."

And Wendy thought about it some more.

"You think Jim Starke's got cold eyes?"

Jennifer actually made a shivering sound, but then laughed.

"God, yes! He's actually scarier than the bigger guy."

Wendy didn't say anything for a long moment.

"I never thought about it," she admitted. "The bigger one with the scar is Mr. Thurman's son, and he probably *is* dangerous, now that you mention it. I'd say he was dangerous when I knew him. But Jim Starke is just a sweet guy."

Jennifer clearly didn't believe it.

"Seriously?"

"My sister Pam used to date him," Wendy went on. "But I think Pam's weirdly jealous about it. Whenever I'd ask about Jim on the phone, she always changed topics. Always. She won't talk about him."

"So he's your sister's boyfriend?"

Wendy shook her head.

"Not really," she said. "Not anymore, at least..."

And then Wendy suddenly turned the big car down an almost entirely overgrown lane, a rutted two-wheel dirt path that dipped down, leading narrowly through tall trees and thick underbrush.

It was a narrow opening that was almost impossible to see from I.C. Boulevard.

"There's no road here!" Jennifer said. "This is a swamp!"

"That it is," her mother agreed.

She followed the path for approximately an eighth of a mile, through open swampy marshland that began on the other side of the underbrush and threatened to spill over at any moment to obliterate what dry ground there was, then back through another stand of silk oak, eucalyptus and black olive trees.

The ground cover was so thick that any number of large reptiles, including alligators and American crocodiles, native to the Florida Everglades, might have been living right there.

"It's okay," Wendy assured her daughter, who was looking more apprehensive by the moment. "I know this place."

"You mean you used to."

"It hasn't changed a bit."

Wendy pointed. A simple tire swing hung forlornly from a giant moss-laden cypress tree just ahead, a mucky small pond slimed over with green beneath it. "I put that up myself. The water was horrible even then. It was a real mess if you fell in."

"My God. So you *were* a tomboy."

Another curving turn past the tree-line brought them to a small trailer camp within a marshy clearing that looked as if the six once road-worthy metallic dwellings in a half-circle had been abandoned to the encroaching wilderness.

The most noticeable of the six was an ancient Airstream, gutted and charred by fire, the hulk standing in a blackened circle of ash that went right up to the narrow trailers on either side, as if only a miracle had stopped the inferno from taking the entire place. Nearby, within the trees, several apparently abandoned junk cars stood at different angles.

"There's no one living here anymore," Jennifer announced.

Wendy, of course, knew better.

"They're here."

And, as if on cue, a huge fat woman, as big as a small house trailer herself, came around the corner of a badly-repainted sky blue Nomad. A makeshift lean-to fashioned out of plywood, tarpaper and tin had been shakily built onto the side of the low trailer, the windows either missing or boarded up both front and back.

The huge woman was possibly in her sixties, with stringy gray hair and a wide mouth missing many teeth, and she carried a large black pot with both hands. Something dark was sloshing around within it.

She suddenly stopped and looked at the big gray Lincoln as if she'd never seen such a wondrous sight in her entire life.

"Who is *that*?" Jennifer wanted to know, actual fear in her voice now.

Wendy took a deep breath.

"Aunt Prudy, I think. It's been awhile."

"Not long enough."

Wendy gave her daughter a quick look. "Now, be nice. We'll stay awhile. We'll talk. And then we'll get over to the I.C. motel ."

And, nodding slowly, her eyes fixed nervously on the huge woman, it was a long moment before Jennifer finally said, "Okay."

The screen door to the bright blue Nomad then opened with a bang and a very old tall skinny man stepped out with a big smile. His long white hair was tied into a loose ponytail that went halfway down his back. He had all his teeth, but they had a greenish-gray cast, evident even from a distance, his large nose and prominent Adam's apple his most noticeable features.

He wore denim shorts with a black leather belt that was too long, a faded black *'Dead Kennedys—Too Drunk To Fuck'* tee shirt, and black plastic thong sandals. His fish-white legs and longish feet had not seen sunlight, by the looks of them, in his entire lifetime.

"So who's that?" the teen asked.

Wendy shut off the car.

She'd immediately recognized the family patriarch, Cuthbert Jamison, even after all the years that had passed by.

"That's my dad...your grandfather." And at Jennifer's horrified look, she added, "Let's get out and meet the family."

Jennifer gave her a look.

"You first."

Wendy hesitated only a moment.

"Fine."

And she swung open the door of her big new Lincoln and stepped out onto the soft, damp ground to finally meet the family she had purposely abandoned, ignored and avoided for over twenty years.

Chapter 31

At Look Out Point, most of the Interception City authorities, meaning fire and law enforcement, had pulled back, following Police Chief Orville Goody's sudden command to simply leave the location.

While waiting for the FDLE forensics crew to arrive, Chief Goody and his son-in-law Ray, however, stayed close, within sight of it all, just in case something, anything, turned up that might implicate either one of them in the murder of either the black FDLE officer or Edna June Thurman.

Up at the actual scene, standing next to the burnt-out Toyota FJ Cruiser, Walter Hightower was on his cell phone, calling in several of the license plates he'd earlier jotted down.

"...and H896B, both in Banyon County," he said. "Lieutenant, those last two plates belong to the two rednecks most likely behind it." Just the thought of those two hick losers made his blood boil. "Elmore probably stopped on the way down, for whatever reason, never got out of this shitbox town…"

He shook his head at the thought.

He'd make certain both of those boys, those killers of his brother, would end up either strapped down to a gurney in the execution chamber up at the Florida State Prison or else would die at the end of his gun.

Two vehicles from Miami's FDLE forensics department suddenly slowed and pulled off the road. Walter gave the crew getting out a quick wave to come on back to the site, but said to Lieutenant Schreiber on the phone:

"Yeah, I'm betting they both got serious prison time. They got that look. And the Interception City Police Chief and his 1st Officer could be a recruiting poster for the Klan. Let's check them out, too…"

Chapter 32

At exactly 8:57 AM, Jim and Thurman Jr. climbed down out of Jim's CJ-5 Jeep in front of the Interception City Police Department. There was one police car parked at the rear of the building, no other cars in the police side of the parking lot in front.

"My poor damn dad," the bigger man said. "I'm going to end up killing somebody over this."

"I believe you," Jim said. "But let's try to be nice to John Pasco. He's a cop, okay?"

Thurman Jr. smiled.

"Okay," he said. "Nice it is."

But then he leaned back into the Jeep, popped open the glove box and took out Jim's 9mm Glock 17. He'd left it there the night before. He checked it, put it into his waistband in back, under his shirt.

"In case he's not nice back."

* * *

Officer John Pasco was sitting at the front desk when they walked in, the only person there. He looked up with surprise when Jim Starke and Horace Thurman Jr. dropped down into the two chairs across from him.

Pasco was a pure redneck, a square-jawed gum-chewing hard-headed cracker to anyone who knew him, his dark hair extra-short so it wouldn't get into his eyes during the many fights he enjoyed getting himself.

But at 9:01 A.M., one hour and one minute past the time his shift would normally end, he found himself instantly wishing he'd left on time. The other officers, normally arriving at 8:00 A.M., were still tied up at the big accident out on CR 823, so he'd stayed over to help out. Also, with everyone out at the accident, he couldn't expect any help if things got ugly, which he imagined would be the case. Whatever these two tough boys wanted, it couldn't be anything but trouble.

Especially with Thurman Jr.'s mother dead out there in her Toyota FJ Cruiser after apparently orally pleasuring some unknown black John Doe literally to death.

"Hello, Officer Pasco," Jim Starke said. "Still out starting bar fights every weekend?"

"What can I do for you?" Pasco asked, ignoring the question.

"You carrying a gun back there?" Thurman Jr. wanted to know right off. "Behind that desk?"

"Jesus—" Jim Starke said. "Thurman. . ."

"I'm asking him nice." And then, "Pasco, you wearing a sidearm?"

Pasco, uncertain where this was heading, but well aware it was nowhere he wanted to end up, simply ignored that question as well and asked again:

"What can I do for you?"

He *was* wearing a sidearm, of course, a single-action Colt Peacemaker in a strap-down holster he'd inherited from his father, a cowboy's piece, in fact, for fast-draw shooting if necessary, but he assumed he'd not live through a shoot-out with either one of these two.

His eyes covertly went to the phone and then, insanely, he knew, to the big gun rack on the far wall. No way was he ever going to reach it, either, if it came to that.

The back of his neck was suddenly damp.

"Just tell me what you want."

Picking fist fights with other drunken redneck bar fighters was one thing, but Jim Starke and Horace Thurman Jr. were terrifying and violent men, and John Pasco (cop or no cop) found himself slowly growing limp with a steadily rising fear, realizing this probably wasn't going to end well.

Whatever the fuck they wanted.

And then Jim Starke asked simply:

"Did you tell Police Chief Orville Goody that the man burned up with Mrs. Thurman was black?"

And Officer John Pasco's eyes widened with genuine surprise. And sudden absolute terror.

He swallowed hard, found that he could barely speak, for he instantly knew he had somehow ended up between two hostile camps, one containing these two probable killers and the other that of Police Chief Orville Goody, a killer in his own right, but one with a badge and the willingness to use it in any manner whatsoever.

"What was that?" he asked. "Say that again, Jim—"

Thurman Jr. shifted in his seat and Pasco flinched, his heart leaping.

"Chief Goody told us the dead man with Mrs. Thurman was black," Jim Starke said. "He said you told him this morning it was a nigger, to use your term, when you found the wreck…"

"He said *what*?"

Jumping Jesus Christ Almighty!

John Pasco thought he might literally pass out from terror if one of the other I.C.P.D. officers didn't show up *right now* and save his lonesome ass from whatever insane mess he was in here!

He hadn't been able to tell any such thing when he first found the wreck, couldn't even, in fact, tell it was Mrs. Thurman in there, except by the license plate finally, after he'd called it in. Only later, back at the front desk in the station and hearing about it over the radio from the other cops at the scene had he even learned the dead man was—or might have been— black.

Now, according to the police chief himself, John Pasco had started the whole fucking black man angle with one early morning phone call!

Holy shit!

"I don't use the word 'nigger' no more," John Pasco got out. "I got nothing against the race, never have..."

Which was when Thurman Jr. finally exploded.

"We don't care about your sensitive fucking nature!" Thurman Jr. jumped up. "What did you tell that fat cocksucker Orville Goody?"

"What did Chief Goody say I said again?"

"What *did* you say?" Jim Starke asked.

"Tell us now," Thurman Jr. said evenly. "Or the next time you're out looking for a bar fight, I'll be there to give you one."

John Pasco took a steadying breath.

"Thurman, I'm a police officer. You can't—"

"Yes, I can."

"Damn, Thurman, I'd never start a fight with you—you'd kill me!"

"We're gonna see."

Officer John Pasco sat silently for a long moment, considering. He looked to the double office doors that said 'Orville P. Goody, Chief of Police' and then made a decision, the only sensible decision he could: to lie!

"I *did* say it was a black man," he started. "When I called the Chief from the scene this morning, I told him that. I didn't realize it was Mrs. Thurman, of course..." To Thurman Jr., he added, "Sorry for your loss, by the way."

Thurman Jr. didn't respond, still standing.

Jim remained seated, but nodded.

"How'd you know the man was black?" he wanted to know.

Pasco shrugged.

"It was just an impression, nothing definite. His features maybe—"

"His features were burned off."

"Maybe the way he was sitting, then..."

Jim smiled at that one.

"He was sitting like a black man?"

John Pasco smiled back, started getting comfortable with his lie, with the fact that Police Chief Orville Goody, his son-in-law Officer Ray Lanyard and the entire I.C. police force would back him up.

"It was *something* about him made me think he was black. Hell, I'm guessing now I was probably dead wrong. Now that I think about it, he could have been a fucking Chinese for all I knew—"

Thurman Jr. suddenly stepped around the front desk and grabbed John Pasco by the throat so tightly the policeman jerked sharply with a strangled cry.

"Are you fucking with us?" he asked.

"He's a cop," Jim Starke mentioned.

"Right."

Black spots were already forming before John Pasco's eyes.

Horace Thurman Jr.'s grip was like an actual steel vise! Jesus, Mary and Joseph, he was about to be strangled to death in the middle of the fucking police station, and what the hell was *that* going to look like in the papers? Yet even with

Thurman Jr.'s right hand so tightly around his throat that he couldn't get a single breath, he knew better than to grab the big man's wrist.

He simply gripped both arms of his chair and waited to die.

And then, at an almost imperceptible nod from Jim Starke, Thurman Jr. loosened his hold just slightly.

"Thurman, I swear to Christ," Pasco got out. "I told Chief Goody the guy was black!"

"The black guy was your idea?" Jim asked.

"Right. I'm so damn sorry."

"You will be, if you're lying," Thurman Jr. said.

And with that he let Officer John Pasco go, then turned and walked out the front door without another word.

Jim Starke stood up.

Pasco sat trying to rub the circulation back into his throat and neck with hands that trembled. Still breathing shakily, he looked to Jim.

"See you at the big reunion tonight," was what Jim said.

And then he too was gone

"Thank you, Lord!" was all Pasco could think to say. He took a couple of deep breaths, letting them out slowly, steadying himself finally.

Then he picked up the phone and dialed Police Chief Orville Goody's private cell phone number.

Chapter 33

Across the intersection at the Thurman home, as Mr. Thurman busied himself fixing all three of them some food, Jim Starke was not surprised to discover his closest friend accepted his mother's death exactly as it appeared.

In other words, that one of the woman's many sexual misadventures had finally resulted in her demise.

"Damn her ass to hell!" Thurman Jr. said again, enraged.

Like a scorpion so insanely angered it ended up stinging itself to death, Thurman Jr. slammed his fist into the solid wooden door leading into the pantry. His knuckles came back bloody but he hammered it again, this time splintering the door in the center.

"Goddamn her!"

Jim Starke watched silently.

"I won't have you saying such things about your mother!" Mr. Thurman Sr. suddenly interjected. "That's enough!"

His son simply stared at him.

"Pop, she whored around this godforsaken town her entire life and you're surprised she died during sex with a stranger?"

"Don't say another word!" the older man said to his son. "I won't hear it!"

Thurman Jr. hit the already splintered pantry door another resounding blow, then stormed off to the rear of the huge old house. A moment later, Jim heard a door slam somewhere in one of the back rooms.

There was a long and uncomfortable silence.

"I'm really sorry about all this, Mr. Thurman," Jim said. "I still can't believe it…"

The older man said nothing for a very long moment, then wearily dropped down into one of the kitchen chairs. He motioned for Jim to sit.

"I've always loved my wife," Mr. Thurman said simply. "But damn me, I did nothing to stop her."

"This isn't your fault—"

But the man simply held up a hand.

"My love for Edna June was all I cared about," he went on. "Even *more*, apparently than I cared about her. If it actually turns out she died having sex with that man, I'll never forgive myself."

"Mr. Thurman, I don't believe Edna June even *knew* the man."

The older man nodded.

"I wish you and Horace would find out," he said. "If her death turns out to be an accident, then so be it. If, however, it isn't an accident. . ."

Jim said, "If it isn't an accident, whoever's responsible will wish they'd died in that wreck instead."

"More than you know," Thurman Jr. suddenly walked back into the kitchen. To his father, he threw out, "Hey, sorry, Pop..."

Mr. Thurman wearily nodded and waved it off. He knew his son well enough.

Jim said, "I was just thinking, if the man in the car really is the missing FDLE officer, where's his car?"

"I was just wondering the same thing," Thurman Jr. said.

"All towed or abandoned cars end up out at Oliver Goody's junkyard."

"Exactly," Thurman Jr. said, nodding. "Oliver and I got into it one time—he thought I wouldn't stomp his nuts into the ground because he had a straight razor (and here he touched at his scar) and because he's the police chief's brother. He was proved wrong on both counts."

"So I remember."

"If he gives us any trouble, I'll stick his head straight up his fat ass."

Jim looked to the bigger man.

"Instead of sticking his head up his ass, what if we surprised him and just asked a few questions?"

Thurman Jr. had to laugh.

"Too fucking easy," he said.

Chapter 34

Police Chief Orville Goody and Officer Ray Lanyard stood in front of Officer John Pasco at the front desk. The Chief was steaming mad.

"Pasco, tell me again—why in hell those two criminal troublemakers aren't behind bars or dead on the floor in here? Did they hold a gun on you the entire time...?"

"They didn't show no guns, Chief," Pasco admitted.

Orville Goody slapped his fat thigh so loudly both officers, John Pasco and Ray Lanyard, jumped.

"Dammit, Officer Pasco, you should've pulled your weapon and shot both those bastards straight through the hearts!"

"Until Thurman made his move, Chief, there was no indication trouble was coming. We're having a conversation when—BANG—it's like I got a goddamn bear trap on my windpipe." He tenderly rubbed his throat at the thought of it. "That Thurman Jr.'s one strong son of a bitch!"

The conversation was making Chief Goody angrier with every moment, his patience just about to snap.

"What'd they want?"

John Pasco swallowed hard at the memory.

"Well...they said I told you the dead man with Mrs. Edna June was black."

He noted that the Chief exchanged a quick glance with Officer Ray, but then both acted as if they were as puzzled as Pasco had been by that particular line of questioning. The Chief looked back to him.

"And what did you tell 'em?"

"I told them I mentioned it to you this morning, that I thought the man was black, just like they said you said."

The Chief nodded.

"Good man."

"So...why'd they say that?"

Orville Goody suddenly threw his arms up to express his annoyance with the entire episode.

"Because they're both insane with grief and confusion," he tried to explain. "Thurman Jr.'s mother dies in a sexual situation with a black man, how's that gonna sit with most white men...?"

And at that moment, Walter Hightower banged in through the front door, then looked to each of them, hard.

"You got big trouble, Chief!" he said. "Our dead officer's got bullet holes in him. Your stupid cracker friends thought they could just throw him in next to a white woman, burn them up so bad no one could tell, but it doesn't work like that—"

"Those boys aren't friends," Officer Ray pointed out.

Walter shot him a dirty look.

"Officer Gomer, shut the fuck up when I'm talking."

He waited a long moment until Ray Lanyard finally looked away, then turned back to the Chief.

"I'm bringing down the whole world on your shithole town. You and your officers are to stay out of my way or I'll arrest every one of you for interfering with an ongoing police investigation. Do you understand that?"

Chief Goody fixed the man with a hard look of his own, but then finally smiled at the situation. It was working out even better than he could have hoped, even though he was furious with Ray for convincing him there'd be nothing left of the bullet holes in the dead black man.

After all, all four slugs *had* passed right on through.

Orville Goody told Walter, "The two rough boys who likely did this are not going to escape the law. For a start, we're arresting Jim Starke and Horace Thurman Jr. for felony assault on a police officer."

Walter scowled. "What new bullshit is this?"

Chief Goody gestured toward John Pasco.

"They tried to murder this officer and I'm going to see 'em both charged with it."

Walter took a good look at Pasco.

"He looks fine to me."

"I was strangled," the man told him.

"You're still breathing—"

"Only by God's good grace and will," Orville Goody intoned. He turned to his officer. "Pasco, I want a written statement from you, right now, specifying the assault and specifying the intent-to-murder nature of the crime."

To which Officer John Pasco suddenly looked stricken at the thought. Terrified, actually. He stood.

"Sorry, Chief," he said. "You got no idea what you're asking. Put me in jail, you want, fire me. Hell, shoot me. I ain't signing no paper against Jim-boy Starke or Thurman Jr.—"

"Goddamn it, Pasco!" Officer Ray said.

"So those two crackers are your friends?' Walter asked the man.

"Hell, no," Officer Ray cut in again. "Pasco's afraid they'll catch him in the dark and cut his throat."

John Pasco gave Ray a look.

"Those boys don't need no dark."

Walter said, "You're an officer of the law."

John Pasco began gathering up his things as he spoke.

"That don't matter to Jim-boy or Thurman Jr. around here. Ask around, you'll see."

He took off his badge, put it on the desk.

"I'm sorry, Chief, but I hereby give you my resignation."

And he walked out the front door.

"I don't believe this," Walter Hightower said.

Chief Orville Goody had to smile again. "The two bad boys that killed your man, that's how most feel—too scared to go against 'em, rather run away than be murdered in cold blood by their likes."

"Why are you so certain it was them?"

The Chief gave him a look of surprise.

"Thurman's mother in a—uh—delicate compromise with a...a member of another race...? You might not like to think it, but folks around here are not likely to overlook such an incident."

Walter exhaled slowly.

"So he kills his own mother?"

Chief Goody shrugged.

"Wouldn't be the first, killing kin over a racial...indiscretion. Or maybe she tried to stop the killing, wasn't intended as the victim. Wouldn't be the first for that, either..."

Walter honestly didn't know what to say, stared at the Chief for a long moment, then looked to Officer Ray, who nodded sagely as if such things happened all the time. Walter had to look away.

From both of the men he considered morons.

He told them, "I need a private office and an Internet hook-up for my laptop."

Chief Orville Goody gave him a big smile as if all was suddenly right with the world.

"Not a problem, Officer Hightower," he said, then to Ray added, "Let's make this man feel right at home."

Which got him a dubious look from Walter.

Chapter 35

Out at the far western edge of town, Oliver Goody's junkyard looked exactly as expected, a high-fenced dirt-packed twelve acres filled with rusted car and truck hulks stacked in a tropical jungle setting.

Two snoozing pit-bulls were tied near the front gate.

Near the back of the grounds, sat a large ramshackle barn, all the doors and windows either boarded over or covered by thick burglar bars. Within, Oliver Goody, as big-boned as his brother, and his large, mean-spirited twenty-three-year-old son, Lukas, pulled a large tarp off a new black Corvette convertible with the top down.

Oliver climbed in behind the wheel.

"Damn," his boy said, impressed. And when his father pulled shut the heavy car door, "Solid."

Oliver started the car with a *VROOM*. It rumbled steadily. He gunned it twice, the racing engine sending a thrill through every inch of him.

"Damn car's better'n our house," he said.

"What we gonna do with it, Daddy...?"

That was the question all right, Oliver reflected.

The black Corvette had become a problem to Oliver the second he'd seen it.

His brother Orville and that pencil-neck Ray Lanyard had yesterday brought the car in and requested he cut it up for scrap and spare parts immediately. Orville told him enough of the shot-dead-black-man story to convince him it would be wise to dispose of the vehicle fast, but Oliver was having serious second thoughts that had started as soon as the two lawmen had driven off .

Oliver Goody had wanted a new black Corvette his entire life.

Of course, he'd never come within hailing distance of such a car. His junkyard, while large, attracted only the average or below-average array of wrecked cars and trucks— nothing as exotic as a Corvette had ever been hauled into the place.

Also, he wasn't insane enough to go off and try to buy one outright. Most folks in Banyon County, and even over in Clewiston, just didn't have the money for such a fancy ride. Such an *expensive* ride.

That this one had belonged to a black man, even a dead one, irked him no end.

"Daddy..." Luka reminded him he was there. "The car...?

But the crackling static of his walkie-talkie stopped him from answering the boy. He pulled it off his belt, hit the button, heard a female voice, "Oliver, couple boys here want to talk to you."

"About what?"

"It's Jim Starke and Thurman Jr."

Olivier swore under his breath, gave Lukas a look.

"I'm heading up front. Better cover this thing back up.

When Oliver Goody walked into his front office, he found Jim Starke and Thurman Jr. waiting for him, Jim standing there with a smile and the larger man leaning against the front counter.

The lone clerical woman the junkyard owner employed stayed near the back of the office, staring down at her desk as if looking for some paperwork she'd misplaced, clearly wanting no part of anything about to happen.

And something definitely was about to.

Thurman Jr.'s reputation *always* preceded him in Interception City.

"What can I do for you boys?" Oliver asked.

Jim told him, "We're looking for a black Corvette you towed in here the last day or so—"

Oliver smirked, just shook his head. He pretended to be busy wiping his hands on a filthy red shop towel.

"Ain't no black Corvette. Or any Corvette."

Thurman Jr. lazily detached himself from the counter he'd been leaning against.

"We're going to take a look around," he said.

"I don't think so," Oliver straightened.

Thurman Jr. gave Jim a look, then turned back to Oliver Goody with a smile that would've chilled anyone who knew him, or even *of* him, to the bone.

* * *

Back at the Interception City Police Department, Walter was getting settled in.

He'd taken his laptop out of its case and was setting it up on a dusty desk in an empty office off to the side when he heard the main phone ring. He casually listened in as Ray answered it.

"I.C. Police," the skinny man in black said. "Officer Ray Lanyard...got it."

When Ray hung up, he told Orville Goody, "Chief, out at Oliver's junkyard, those two damn troublemakers are out there right now starting some damn thing about that black sports car—"

Which caused Walter Hightower to walk right out to them.

"I'm going with you," he announced.

He saw Chief Orville Goody exhale after giving Officer Ray a disgusted look at apparently disclosing that information, but the big man then turned and nodded tightly to Walter.

"You can follow us out," Chief Goody agreed.

"Let's go."

Chapter 36

Tommy and Eugene Luercher lived to give other people pain.

First cousins, they worked out of Miami, a city plenty mean enough to keep them both busy. For mostly small change, they put the serious hurt on deadbeats, welchers, other petty criminals and the occasional ex-spouse or two.

For a little more, they'd make it permanent.

Ten miles outside of Interception City, they were heading in from the east, driving a stolen 1998 Ford Taurus station wagon on a narrow back road that cut through the saw-grass swamp.

Tommy was at the wheel, a handsome and muscular 28-year-old jock in blue-mirror sunglasses with a large gold chain around his neck. Professionally, he specialized in the use of a simple pair of standard hardware store pliers, although he did prefer the rubber-handle-grip variety.

Of course, he also carried a 9mm Sig Sauer.

"How's Joey?" he asked. "You heard from him?"

His speed-freak-thin cousin, Eugene at twenty-three, was slumped down in the other seat, eyes closed.

"Huh--"

Eugene wasn't much of a talker, yet believed himself to be the educated one due to a Psychology 101 course he was allowed to briefly monitor during one of his many stays at the Glade Correctional Institution in Belle Glade. In pegged-leg dirty jeans and an oversized *Ron Jon's* tee shirt, he looked even taller and skinnier than he really was.

"Hey," Tommy said again, with obvious irritation. "Our other fucking cousin? How's Joey doing?"

"We won't know until the jury's picked."

Tommy nodded to himself.

Short-tempered on even the best of days, his younger cousin never failed to annoy the shit out of him with that fucking attitude of his, never answering a straightforward question with a simple straightforward answer.

"What's the asshole motel she's checking into?" he asked then. "The lady we're supposed to do?"

Eugene barely stirred.

"I got it written down somewhere. Let me dig it out when we get there."

Tommy nodded agreeably.

"Sure, no problem."

But he reached over and grabbed Eugene's narrow knee with such brutal force that the razor-thin young man straightened with a yelp, eyes opening wide as he half-raised out of the seat like a writhing wire coat-hanger.

"Fuck, fuck, fuck...!"

Tommy released his grip.

Eugene dropped back into the seat like a wet rag, panting for breath and desperately rubbing his knee. Then he dug out a scrap of paper, squinted at his own terrible pencil-manship.

"The fucking I.C. Motel. She's going to some school reunion tonight, got a kid with her, gotta look like a robbery gone wrong, two bullets in the head, grab whatever paperwork she's got—no harm to the kid, not even supposed to see us."

He gave his older cousin a petulant look.

"Happy, now?"

"Yeah, I am. Thanks."

"You almost broke my goddamn knee. You're a scary man."

Tommy nodded again.

"I'm supposed to be."

Knowing what was to come, Eugene shook his head again.

Tommy loved the work, that was obvious, but to Eugene it was all merely a job. It was nothing to get excited about, certainly nothing to look forward to. Tommy, on the other hand, *lived* for it.

If he'd had an actual soul, Eugene Luercher might've felt sorry for the woman they were driving over to Interception City to kill.

Chapter 37

Driving over to his brother Oliver's junkyard in the squad car with FDLE Officer Walter Hightower right on their tail, Police Chief Orville Goody was so mad he was half-tempted to just stop the car and stomp the hell of his idiot son-in-law riding next to him.

And now the weasely son of a bitch was whining once again.

"But, Chief..." he complained.

"I told you, Ray, shut up. This is all your fault, so you're doing it—Pasco says a word, we're facing the death penalty. You got to make it look like Jim Starke or Thurman Jr. did it. They already attempted murder on Pasco once, but this time they succeed."

"They're gonna have a hell of an alibi if they're in our jail when Pasco dies," Ray pointed out.

"That's why they're not going to be arrested."

Officer Ray looked to him, perplexed.

"What if they find that Corvette...?"

"We'll deal with it then," Chief Goody refused to even look at the man. "For now, use that pathetic brain of yours to figure out killing ex-I.C. Police Officer John Pasco." He thought about it for several more seconds, then added, "Get your sawed-off shotgun from home."

"Okay."

"And don't say a word about *any* of this to Virginia."

Officer Ray looked away, out his window, suddenly seeming uneasy.

The Chief shook his head, knowing it was probably already too late. The man Virginia had married was absolutely hopeless.

"Ray, did you tell my daughter any of this?" he wanted to know. "Anything at all?"

Officer Ray finally turned back to him, then shook his head.

"Not a word," he insisted. "I'm not a retard idiot."

Orville Goody kept his eyes on the road.

Yeah, right, he thought to himself.

Chapter 38

After checking into the I.C. Motel, Wendy parked the big gray Lincoln directly in front of their room.

The motel itself was a long masonry-block one-story building claiming HBO, clean sheets, and a phone in each of the 14 rooms. At 12:45 on a Saturday afternoon, the place was mostly deserted, only four cars and a single pick-up truck in evidence.

A young heavyset maid in shorts and a tee-shirt was working from a linen cart, listlessly making her way from room to room in the almost unbearable heat. The cracked asphalt surface of the parking lot was nearly molten, the woman's tennis shoes making little sticky sounds as she walked.

Anyone barefoot would clearly end up with third degree burns.

The faded red *Coca Cola* thermometer fastened outside the office showed it was 92 degrees in the shade. The humidity was anybody's guess. There wasn't even a hint of a breeze.

Wendy and Jennifer pulled their suitcases out of the trunk. Then Wendy grabbed her burgundy leather briefcase.

Inside the room, they were both pleased to discover the air conditioner was cranking full blast, welcome relief from even the short walk from the car. It was a clean enough place, two double beds, a long pressboard shelf with an older television on it along one wall, and heavy blackout drapes that were closed, causing Wendy to have to search for the light switch.

The switch on the wall did nothing.

She left the door partially open, set her briefcase on the shelf, moved to the small table lamp on the nightstand between the beds. It went on, but the dim light that filtered through the opaque-paper shade did little to brighten the room.

"Mother, it's broad daylight outside," Jennifer said after tossing her suitcase onto the bed near the door. "We'll go blind in the dark like this."

And the girl pulled open the blackout drapes, and the regular drapes behind them, to discover two men standing right at the window, a tall skinny one and a shorter more muscular man wearing blue mirror sunglasses.

Chapter 39

Tommy and Eugene Luercher.

"What do these two weirdo's want?" the teen, annoyed, loudly asked about the men at the window. "Fuck off!"

"Jennifer, lock the door!"

Wendy reached for the room phone, got her hand on it and hit the '0' button on the faceplate.

But before her daughter could push the door closed all the way, the muscular man easily forced it open and, holding a big pistol in his hand, stepped into the room with them. His skinny, strung-out-looking friend followed.

"I called 9-1-1..." Wendy said, holding up the phone.

Tommy Luercher quickly stepped around the first bed, roughly grabbed Wendy's arm, then pulled the phone to his ear.

"Front desk..." the voice on the other end said.

He hung up the phone, pressed the 9mm Sig Sauer he held under Wendy's chin. Out of the corner of her eye, she could see that the skinny man was holding Jennifer by one arm, a thin kitchen-type knife held to her throat.

"My purse is on the bed there," Jennifer managed.

"Shut up," Tommy told her.

"She's right," Wendy added. "Just take our money and go."

In response, Tommy suddenly backhanded Wendy across the face with the gun, the jarring blow snapping her head back. She dropped to one knee between the two double beds.

Jennifer cried out, but was caught short by the other man's sharp blade pressing into her throat, making her rise up on her toes.

Tommy shook his head, exhaled slowly. Fuck. This was *not* how it was all supposed to go.

"Eugene, now what the hell…?"

"Thanks for using my name. Tommy!"

The muscular man in the sunglasses didn't seem overly concerned.

"It don't matter now," he pointed out. "They both gotta go."

Eugene could see that, too, nodded thoughtfully.

"Right, right, but not here," he said. "We do the mom, take the kid with us, finish it far away. She ran off, got run over maybe, not our fault."

"Sounds right." He pointed the gun at Wendy, still down on one knee. "You, stay right there."

Wendy obeyed.

She knew better than to do anything foolish. Yet. She looked to her daughter, saw Jennifer was so scared the girl had her eyes tightly shut. It took everything she had to just stay where she was.

"Why are you doing this?" she wanted to know.

Then watched as Tommy Luercher opened her briefcase, pulled out a handful of paperwork, the ledger book and the corporate checkbook, all of it from her cable TV show. He looked at it, then stuffed it all back inside.

"Leonard…" she realized. "That goddamn son of a bitch."

Jennifer said, "My dad's a federal judge—if you hurt us, he'll make the FBI hunt you down!"

Which got a smirky laugh from both Tommy and Eugene.

"Honey, that's funny," the skinny man informed her. "Your father's the one paying us to get all those papers back, make sure your mother doesn't live long enough to complain about it—"

"You're crazy!" the girl said. But then, maybe realizing, "Mother…?"

"It was only your mom supposed to never wake up," he went on. "But you whipped open that shade, so now you're in the same heap of shit…"

Wendy said, "Just shut up and leave her alone."

Eugene smirked again.

"I wasn't talking to you," he said. "You're lucky they got DNA these days or we'd be having a lot more fun with both of you."

"God, you're a pig."

Tommy laughed.

"I don't think you're turning her on."

Still keeping the knife tightly against the young girl's throat, Eugene squeezed the back of Jennifer's jeans, causing her to suddenly shake violently. "This looks like the hot one to me," he said.

Wendy, enraged, stood up.

"Keep your hands off her, you fucking weasel!"

She put her foot up on the bed, actually was ready to come across it and try killing them both, held back only when Eugene pressed the tip of the blade into her daughter's throat until a thin trickle of blood suddenly appeared.

The man smiled evilly at her.

"Lady, you're giving me a real bone on here, but shut the fuck up."

"Mom…!"

"I know, sweetie. Just don't move."

Tommy nodded agreement.

"Good advice. Everyone stays put."

He snapped the gun back into the holster under the back of his shirt. To Eugene, he said, "Open the door more, try to look like a family on vacation. I'm going to put this case in the car, then we'll finish up."

Eugene nodded, reached behind him with his free hand and opened the door wider, the knife blade still at Jennifer's throat. He held the door open with his back, kept Jennifer to the inside so she couldn't be seen from outside.

Tommy said to Wendy, with a laugh, "When I get back, you and I are going to make a big mess in here."

He walked past Eugene and the girl, casually walked out to the Ford Taurus station wagon, which was parked directly across the lot. It faced the room, backed against a cement block wall.

From where she stood between the beds, Wendy watched him open the back driver's side door of the car and put in her briefcase. She glanced at Eugene. His wary eyes never left her, his blade still tight against Jennifer's throat.

Wendy looked back to the parking lot, forced herself to not look at Eugene or her daughter.

When Tommy slammed the car door, she said, "What the...?"

Eugene turned only slightly to see. A fraction of a second to look back.

But Wendy, foot still up on the bed, had already slipped her small .32 Beretta Tomcat semi-automatic out of her ankle holster and shot Eugene through the left eye with a *bang* so loud Jennifer jumped with a yelp.

Tommy Luercher froze beside the station wagon.

Eugene dropped to his knees, still somehow gripping the knife, and Wendy moved fast to the doorway. She shot the skinny killer point-blank in the forehead, the impact slamming the back of his shattered skull into the door with a bloody thump.

"Get out of the way!" Wendy screamed at her daughter, pushing her back. "Damn it, get down!"

As Tommy grabbed behind him for his gun, Wendy fired two more shots, one screaming off the side of the Ford Taurus, the other catching the man in the side, a bloody mark appearing on his shirt beneath his rib cage.

Even from where she stood, she could hear him groan.

He fired wildly as he yanked open the car door, his shot taking out the plate glass front window of their motel room.

Wendy shot him again, through the driver's side window he stood behind, the safety glass spider-webbing as the slug tore into Tommy's left side in almost exactly the same spot.

"You fucking bitch!"

He fired once more, hitting nothing, then jumped into the old station wagon, started it, and floored it out of the parking lot with barely squealing tires.

Wendy shot at him yet again, shattered his driver-side mirror before the car finally disappeared down the road.

"Damn."

She'd wanted the muscular man dead, dead in front of her own eyes, deader than dried dogshit on a hot Sunday afternoon, a phrase she'd heard many times growing up in Interception City.

Today, it seemed entirely appropriate.

Jennifer suddenly was hanging onto her, hysterical but clearly relieved. Wendy slid her .32 into her jeans pocket, held onto the girl, kissed her forehead, slowly managed to calm her down.

"It's okay, Jen," she assured her. "It's okay now."

The shattered mess that used to be Eugene Luercher was still slumped against the motel room door.

"Don't look at him," Wendy advised her teen daughter. Then, "Did you know I had my gun?"

Jennifer, shakily, gave her mother a look.

"Mother, I'm not an idiot—when *don't* you have your gun?"

Chapter 40

Out at Oliver Goody's junkyard, Jim and Thurman Jr. walked through the many rows of wrecked and flattened cars and trucks. Oliver Goody himself saw fit to follow them; helplessly, it turned out.

His hefty son, Lukas, and one of Oliver's young employees, Danny, looked on as well, but kept their distance.

"Goddamn it!" Oliver had yelled out more than once, to no avail. "You boys are trespassing!"

This last time, Thurman Jr. turned to face him.

"I told Jim I wouldn't stick your head up your fat ass, Oliver. Don't make me a liar."

Jim, spotting the large junkyard barn near the back of the 12 acre grounds, pointed and asked, "What's in there?"

But before Oliver Goody could answer, or even choose not to, I.C. Police Chief Orville Goody and Officer Ray pulled into the parking lot alongside the razor wire-topped fence and stopped. Right behind them, Walter Hightower's unmarked FDLE car pulled in and stopped as well.

Seeing them all park, Oliver called out to Jim and Thurman Jr., "Now we'll see who's in charge here..."

Chief Goody, Officer Ray and Walter Hightower got out of their cars, walked around the front office and then through it, finally arriving where Oliver Goody was standing. At the same time, Jim and Thurman Jr. kept walking until they reached the barn.

"You boys, come on back over here," Orville Goody called out. "Hey!"

"Be right there, Chief," Jim called back, but without stopping or even turning to face the man.

At the large barn, there was a heavy padlock on the sliding door. Thurman Jr. pulled at it, found it was locked. He scooped up a piece of scrap iron and easily pried off the entire hasp.

They he pushed open the sliding door and walked in.

Although the overhead lights were off and the windows were covered, it was easy enough in the light from the open door to make out a vehicle sitting there, covered with a large tarp.

"What do you think that is?" Jim asked his friend.

"This junkyard motherfucker's in on it."

Which was when Chief Orville Goody, Officer Ray, Oliver Goody and Walter walked in, the FDLE officer leading the way.

Walter stared at the tarp a long moment before he finally stepped forward and dragged it off, revealing the black Corvette convertible.

"I'll be damned," was all he said.

"Is that your dead officer's car?" Jim wanted to know. "Officer...?"

Walter turned around to face everyone, in the same motion sliding out his big .44 Magnum. He let them all get a very good look at it.

"I don't know what's going on," he said. "But we're going to clear it up."

Orville Goody was shocked.

"Are you out of your mind?" he asked. "I'm the Chief of Police—"

Walter Hightower gave him a murderous look.

"Chief, I want you to take out your handcuffs and handcuff this man," he said, meaning his brother, Oliver. "Do it and don't fuck with me. I will shoot your ass, I will shoot his ass, I will shoot all your asses, if you even look at me crooked."

Oliver looked to his brother. "Orville...?!"

Walter thumbed back the hammer of the big .44, for emphasis. He knew how to make a point.

"Shut your fucking mouth. You've got a stolen car in your barn belonging to a murdered FDLE officer. You're so goddamn under arrest—"

"Officer Hightower," Chief Goody said quietly, with a knowing sideways look to Jim and Thurman Jr. "These two bad boys knew right where to look."

Walter turned his attention away from Oliver and back to the police chief, then studied Jim and

Thurman Jr. for a very long moment. Finally, he had to laugh.

Which surprised them all.

"That right, boys?" Walter asked them. "You those stupid rednecks I hear about, so stupid you'd kill a police officer, knowing it's the death penalty here in Florida, hide his car in the police chief's brother's barn, then lead an officer from the Florida Department of Law Enforcement to that barn...?"

He could only shake his head.

"You really *that* stupid?"

Jim met his look. "I told you, we're not your problem."

"I'm not sure who's my problem," Walter admitted. "But you two still got that real bad 'need to be in prison' look, so watch it." He looked to Thurman Jr. with a particularly nasty smile. "I ain't forgot the 'Officer Nigger,' either."

"Sorry," the big man said.

Which greatly surprised both Jim and Walter.

The FDLE officer shook his head, then motioned for Chief Goody to take Oliver Goody outside.

"Move your piece of shit brother out of here," he told the man. "When I get back to the jail, I'm going to have a talk with him. And with you."

He turned away, took out his cell phone, got his superior on the line.

"Lieutenant, I found the impound car—"

Behind him, Oliver was starting to panic.

"Orville, you can't let this happen. It ain't right!"

Walter turned back.

"Chief Goody, I told you to get him out of my sight."

The police chief began moving his handcuffed brother along, tried to quiet him. As they passed by, Jim heard him tell the man:

"Oliver, we'll talk. It'll all work out."

"It'll all work out," Officer Ray added.

"Ray, shut up," the chief told him.

Jim said to the handcuffed man, "We're gonna talk to you, too, Oliver. But you're not going to like it."

Which got a startled look from Oliver and stopped Orville. The chief of police turned to Jim and Thurman Jr. with an angry look.

"Are you threatening my brother?"

Walter put his phone away, watched as Jim silently met the police chief's fierce gaze.

"You worthless son of a bitch," Orville finally sputtered when Jim said nothing further. "We don't take that shit off white trash or niggers!" Then, realizing, to Walter, "My apologies...these boys got me so riled."

Walter walked between Jim and Orville Goody.

"Whoa, is there trouble down here on the plantation? Chief Goody, put your brother in a cell until I get there. Now."

To which Orville exhaled tightly, they abruptly moved Oliver Goody along. Officer Ray followed right behind.

Walter turned back to the black Corvette, studied it, then looked back to Jim and Thurman

Jr., his very first suspects, after all, in the murder of his brother.

"I'm missing something here."

"We all are," Jim told him. "Let's talk at lunch. I'm starved."

At the FDLE officer's surprised look, Thurman Jr. threw in, "It'll be fun. But don't forget to bring your gun."

Chapter 41

Orlando

Suspended Federal judge Leonard Johnson stood in a long line at *Pollo Tropical*, a fast food Caribbean chicken place, talking on his cell phone. He'd turned away from the line, hoping no one could overhear what had turned into a very unpleasant conversation.

"I can't," he said in an urgent whisper. "I just got out on bail for violating my restraining order. And I don't have $25,000 in cash!"

There was only a brief silence on the line.

"Your goddamn wife killed my cousin!" Tommy Luercher exploded. "You're gonna get down here with my money!"

The hired killer was so loud on the phone that the other patrons looked to Leonard uneasily. The judge finally swore, then stepped out of line, moving over to a far corner of the busy restaurant.

"I don't see how I can get down there…"

"I'm going to fucking kill you, your honor! Seriously. We're talking felony murder, both of us."

"I'm familiar with the concept," Leonard pointed out. "Calm down."

"Your bitch of a wife put two bullets in me!"

Leonard took a deep breath and asked about the most important part. At least, most important to him.

"Did you get the papers, at least?"

"I got the damn papers, the check book and all that. But Eugene's dead, your wife and daughter know what I look like, I got two bullet holes in me and by now the police are looking for us both—"

"Both?" the judge cut in, thinking the man's wounds and blood loss must be making him delusional. "What have I got to do with this?"

He heard Tommy laugh.

"Felony murder, remember? Eugene told 'em the whole story. You're about to become a wanted man."

"Jesus…"

"What are you driving?" Tommy wanted to know. "Your honor…!"

"A—uh—black Lincoln."

"Your wife's high school reunion tonight, back of the parking lot, 8 o'clock. I'll find you. Have my money or expect to be dead."

Leonard couldn't see the point in arguing.

"It's in my best interest to help you get away," he said.

"You got that right," Tommy said. "But first I'm gonna make sure your wife wishes she never met me."

"I'm certain she already wishes it…"

He heard Tommy Luercher hang up. He exhaled slowly, put away his cell phone, then got back into line.

Chapter 42

Interception City

With a disgusted sigh, Chief Goody turned away from putting his own brother, Oliver, into one of the two cells at the back of the police department offices. Oliver, of course, was not happy with the circumstances.

"Like I told you, I'll handle this," Orville told him. "Just give me a little time."

Which didn't quite appease his brother, but at least quieted him down a bit. When Orville walked out into the front office, he discovered Officer Billy Jordan walking in with Wendy Jamison-Johnson and her daughter, Jennifer.

"Got 'em both, Chief," Jordan said, standing by.

Orville Goody studied Wendy for a long moment.

"So..." he said slowly. "Wendy Jamison. Thought you'd never be caught dead back in Interception City..."

"This is crazy," Wendy said. "That man tried to kill us. And his partner got away!"

The police chief nodded thoughtfully.

"Got no one saw a partner, bunch of shooting and a man shot once through the eye, point blank again through the forehead..." He gave her a dim smile. "Not so sure that's self-defense."

Jennifer blurted, "My mom saved our lives!"

"Saying it don't necessarily make it so."

Officer Billy then put Wendy's .32 Beretta on the desk.

"There's the weapon used..."

Wendy could not believe it.

"I'm a Federal judge's wife," she said. "I was. There have always been threats, or at least the possibility of un-nice people."

"But this time your husband sent 'em," he said, having heard the story related to Billy Jordan at the scene. "The un-nice people, to kill you and his own daughter to get the paperwork from your television show?"

Wendy rolled her eyes.

"Like I told Billy here, the partner took my briefcase with him. That's what he was looking for. They weren't supposed to hurt Jennifer."

At that, Officer Jordan nodded, but got a sharp look from Chief Goody.

Jennifer, at that point, began silently crying.

"God. Daddy! What was he thinking?"

Wendy put her arm around her daughter, pulled her closer. To the I.C. police chief, she said: "I'm meeting with the State Attorney on Monday. My ex-husband doesn't want that to happen."

Which suddenly gave Orville Goody pause.

The State Attorney up in Tallahassee was not someone he wanted to get crosswise with. He nodded again, thoughtfully again, as if seriously considering just how to handle the matter. Fairly, that is.

"Officer Jordan," he started with a smile. "Let's get these folks something to drink. This is gonna take a while…"

Chapter 43

Officer Ray pulled into the long gravel driveway of their trailer home, but was greatly surprised to nearly run into Virginia backing out in her little S-10 pickup. Seeing each other at the last minute as both cleared the wide curve, they slammed on their brakes at the same time.

"Virginia!" Ray yelled as he lowered his window.

His skinny teen wife hopped out of her white Chevy pick-up, left it running, and ran up to his window.

"I'm heading over to Clewiston to shop," she told him. "Back on out."

"Gotta pick up one of my guns," Officer Ray said.

He studied her young form, openly liked what he saw, but then shook his head with a quiet sigh.

"Not off to meet another black man on the Internet...?" he had to ask.

"Ray, I told you what that was about. And I told you, I'm going shopping."

But what she knew, and what her husband didn't, was that her over-stuffed suitcase and many of her most treasured personal items were jammed into the floor-space and on the passenger seat of the small truck.

Virginia Lanyard was getting out.

"I won't be long," she promised him.

But instead of backing out, Officer Ray gave her a dirty grin.

"Let's go back inside," he suggested. "I got something to show you, don't think it can wait..."

She gave him a look.

"Ray, can't we do this when I get back?"

He shook his head in that way that always annoyed the hell out of her, acting as if he either owned her or, at the least, was her boss.

"No, inside for now," he said. "You can head over to Clewiston after."

He motioned impatiently for her to get back into her S-10 and pull it on back to the trailer. She looked at him as if deciding something, but then finally nodded and slowly walked back to her pick-up

Chapter 44

At the screen door of the Alligator Pit, Walter Hightower looked at the Confederate flags and decals on many of the parked cars and trucks, then stared at the part of the sign which said: "No Negroes Please."

He glanced back to Jim and Thurman Jr. with irritation.

"I don't like you people," he said. "By that I mean, dumb-ass redneck peckerwoods in general and you two in particular."

"We might grow on you." Jim said.

"Don't count on it."

All three of them stepped inside, then stopped in the doorway.

As might be expected, the place was half-filled with hard-boiled lunch customers, male and female, some eating, some drinking, but all of them looking up at the trio entering at that moment.

Big Jeff was behind the long counter. He was serving sandwiches and drinks, helping out Pam. Both of them stopped and stared as well.

In the background, the low wail of country music could be heard.

Walter nodded to himself, had to smile.

"So this is Redneck Heaven..."

Thurman Jr. laughed.

"Maybe this *will* turn out to be fun."

Walter just gave him a look.

* * *

Near downtown Interception City, the older Ford Taurus station wagon was parked on a side street near a vacant lot, the long bullet scar down its side and the shattered rear view mirror merely causing it to fit in better as a local vehicle.

Tommy was slumped against the driver's door, a black blood pool on the seat, watching the I.C. Police Department from just far away to not be noticed. He was in pain, great pain, but he had business on his mind for that evening.

Business and revenge.

* * *

Jim and Thurman Jr. sat on each side of Walter at the counter, waiting for either Pam or Big Jeff to approach them. Big Jeff was pointedly ignoring them, but Walter gave the man a smile anyway, got a scowl in return.

He turned to Jim.

"So, your police chief knew our dead officer was black, even though the county coroner couldn't tell?"

Jim nodded.

"He claims a cop, John Pasco, told him."

"I met Officer John Pasco, briefly—he quit the force rather than sign paperwork against either of you." And, at Jim's surprised look, Walter asked, "What is it about you two?"

Jim decided to ignore the question, instead said, "Pasco will be at the reunion tonight. We'll talk to him there."

"No, *I'll* talk to Pasco."

Big Jeff finally walked over, stood before them with barely controlled rage.

"Nice sign out front," Walter said.

"I thought maybe you couldn't read," the owner said. "I'm not a fan of the African-American persuasion…"

Jim looked up.

"Persuasion. That's a new word for you, isn't it, Jeff?"

Big Jeff gave him an annoyed look, but didn't respond. Thurman Jr. smiled. To Walter, he said:

"I knew you'd fit right in."

Walter looked back to Big Jeff.

"Will there be trouble at this here lunch counter, Mr. Bartender?"

"No trouble." He motioned. "Pam, please wait on these gentlemen."

He walked away. At a nearby table, several large redneck bullies shifted around nervously, talking and casting baleful glances at Walter.

Pam walked over, put down three stained single-page menus.

"Jim, what do you think you're doing?" she asked. "Shouldn't the police be standing by...?"

"They *are* standing by."

He motioned to Walter and Walter opened his sport coat, revealing the big .44 Magnum and his FDLE badge. Pam snatched up the menus.

"Sweet tea and three tuna salad sandwiches, it is."

She walked away.

Walter leaned back slightly, casually looked around.

"Nice friendly place," he said. Noting the straight-razor scar across Thurman Jr.'s nose, he asked, "Cut yourself shaving?"

Thurman Jr. smiled.

"I got this from the man you arrested. Oliver Goody. He spent three months in the hospital." He gave it some thought. "Obviously, I should have finished it."

"The police chief claims you murdered your own mother," Walter said. "For... consorting with a black man."

Thurman Jr. merely looked to him then, Walter meeting his gaze. Finally, Walter said, "Right."

Jim said, "Look. We've got Thurman's dead mother and you've got a dead police officer..."

"A dead brother," Walter clarified.

Jim misunderstood.

"A black police officer."

"No, he's my brother. Elmore."

And Jim and Thurman Jr. just stared at him.

Chapter 45

Within the tight confines of Officer Ray's and Virginia's bedroom in their single-wide trailer, a shotgun blast blew the young wife's computer monitor to smithereens.

"Ray, for God's sake!" Virginia cried out.

Her husband reloaded his sawed-off double-barreled shotgun without answering. He then blasted the remains of the computer and monitor with both barrels, the sound deafening in the trailer.

He reloaded again.

"Ray! What are you doing?!"

"I don't *know* what I'm doing," the man admitted, breathing hard. "You make me so goddamn crazy!"

"My dad'll kill you."

"You just be waiting when I get back," he told her. "I'll decide what to do with you then."

And he went out the door, locking it behind him in case anyone showed up at the trailer for whatever reason.

Virginia, finally alone, was handcuffed to the bed in just her panties, her right eye swollen and black from where Officer Ray had hit her. The suitcase from her S-10 was turned upside down, her stuff scattered, their home phone yanked out of the wall and gone.

She listened, finally heard Officer Ray's car start. And leave.

She pulled hard at the handcuff, nearly pulled her bones apart, but the metal bracelet holding her didn't give in the least. Neither did the thick headboard post of their bed.

Trapped.

* * *

Wendy and Jennifer sat across the desk from Chief Orville Goody and Officer Billy Jordan.

"Tell it from the beginning one more time," the police chief said.

"I need to call my attorney," Wendy said. She hadn't bothered earlier because she was so clearly in the right, but it was getting ridiculous. And who knew *what* these idiots might come up with? "Right now."

Orville Goody looked to her, nodded, then handed across the cell phone he'd earlier taken from her.

"That's your right," he said. "Although you are not, and have not been, placed under arrest."

Wendy smiled grimly, punched in the number.

"And I don't intend to be."

Chapter 46

At the Alligator Pit, Jim, Thurman Jr. and Walter all smiled to her as Pam put down their tuna salad sandwiches, with potato chips, gave them a dirty look, and then walked away without a word.

Walter glanced at his sandwich, looked to Jim beside him. Jim switched sandwiches with him.

"If there's anything weird in it, I'm sure I've had worse…"

Walter noticed a huge, fierce-looking red-headed man sitting with two other men who might be his younger, or at least smaller, brothers. Walter nodded to him, smiled, got a startled look in return.

The huge red-headed man said something to the men sitting with him, started to stand but was clearly convinced to sit back down. Walter nodded again.

Then he motioned Big Jeff over.

"What…?"

Walter asked, "So, Mr. bartender, who you figure's the baddest motherfucker in here. It's gotta be me, right?"

Big Jeff didn't answer, so angry he was red-faced.

"Boy—" Walter started, loud enough for all to hear, "I asked you a question. Who do you think's the baddest motherfucker in here?" He glanced over to the huge redheaded man at the table. "It's that big man right there, ain't it?" He admitted, "He looks bad."

The huge man wanted to get up, that was clear, but he held his place.

Big Jeff looked to Jim, appealed to him.

"Jimmy...?

But Jim merely shrugged. Walter, after all, was the law.

Thurman Jr. laughed, turned around to see who Walter was talking about. He made eye contact with the big man, who then all too casually looked away, a fact not missed by Walter Hightower.

He gave Thurman Jr. a much closer look.

To Big Jeff, still standing there, he said, "Maybe I was wrong. Is that big man over there the baddest motherfucker in here or not?" He waited a second, then pressed the issue, "Or not?"

"Fuck you."

Walter smiled.

"Finally, a conversation. I was thinking you didn't like me."

Big Jeff gave the man back a smile of his own.

"Come in here on your own some night and we'll have a conversation, all right—
out back."

Walter considered it.

"I might do that," he said. "But I'll ask you again: who's the baddest motherfucker in here?" He looked to Thurman Jr. beside him. "It's this scarred-up redneck to my left, isn't it? Got all the other hard-ass rednecks in here all nervous."

Thurman Jr. laughed.

Big Jeff said to Walter, "Eat and get the hell out of my place."

And then he disappeared into the back.

Walter turned to Thurman Jr., who shook his head. He then turned back to Jim on the other side.

"But you could kick your buddy's redneck ass if you had to—right?"

Just starting something to see where it'd go.

Jim ignored him but Thurman Jr. asked, "You sure you're a real cop?"

Walter just patted his badge.

"Let's all go have a talk with Chief Goody," Jim suggested. "And his piece-of-shit brother."

Walter stood.

"I'll have the talk. You pay for lunch."

Jim put down the money as he and Thurman Jr. stood. Big Jeff came back out and made a show of throwing Walter's plate and glass into the trash bin.

"Bet it was a chipped one," Walter said, meaning the plate.

"I'll be seeing you," Big Jeff said.

Walter nodded, finger-shot the man.

The huge red-headed man finally stood, walked up to Walter. Jim and Thurman Jr. stepped back. Walter met the much wider and taller redneck's hard gaze.

If the FDLE officer was afraid, he wasn't showing it.

"I want you to know," the bigger man said, "I got no problem with you, not in here or anywhere else. No reason to. That's all."

And he walked back to his seat.

"I'll be damned," Walter said.

"See?" Jim said to him. "You're already making new friends."

Chapter 47

Ex-I.C. Police Officer John Pasco was peeling potatoes at the kitchen sink, standing in front of the large bay kitchen window.

He'd surprised himself by quitting the force that morning, but he knew he'd done the right thing in the long run. Police Chief Goody had somehow gotten into a big mess over that wreck with Edna June Thurman and the supposed black man out at Look Out Point that morning.

And, for whatever obscure reason, Pasco felt the Chief was trying to drag him into the middle of it.

It made no sense, but as far as John Pasco was concerned, he'd head over to Clewiston in the next couple of days and apply to their police force. He knew an officer there he was certain would recommend him.

Pasco's live-in girlfriend, Myra, called out from the other room, "John, I told you I'd do that..."

Pasco didn't even look up.

"I don't mind," he told her. "I gotta bunch of stuff to be thinking about. This helps—"

"I always said Chief Goody was a very bad man."

Pasco nodded to himself.

"I know."

A shotgun blast through the kitchen window knocked down John Pasco. In the shock of the impact, Pasco thought he heard Myra cry out.

"Myra!" he barely managed. "Run!"

He lay sprawled on the bloody floor, discovered he couldn't move. From the other room, he heard his hysterical girlfriend call out, "John, where's your gun?!"

A second later, the back door was kicked in and Officer Ray Lanyard stepped into the kitchen with his sawed-off double-barreled shotgun.

Pasco looked up to him, felt sudden relief.

"Ray, thank God! Somebody shot me!"

Officer Ray raised the shotgun to finish the job but Myra suddenly stepped into the kitchen doorway with Pasco's huge Colt Peacemaker service revolver held shakily in both hands. She'd managed to pull back the hammer and then pulled the trigger, just like John had shown her.

The big gun went off but kicked high in her hands, and she missed.

Officer Ray swung around and, shocked to see the girl was both young and black, blasted her off her feet with the shotgun.

"No! You fucking bastard!" Pasco cried out. He was gasping for breath, couldn't stop shaking. "Myra, no!"

Officer Ray stepped over to Myra's body to make certain she was dead, looked around, then reloaded both barrels of his shotgun. He put both spent shells into his pocket, moved back to the moaning Pasco.

"Real sorry about your woman, John," he said, sincerely. "I figured you'd be alone...never knew she was colored."

Pasco looked up to him with pleading eyes.

"What are you *doing*?" he wanted to know.

Officer Ray stood over him with both barrels pointed straight down.

"Again, sorry, John—Police Chief Goody's orders."

And Officer Ray pulled both triggers.

Chapter 48

Jim and Thurman Jr. pulled up in front of the Interception City Police Department in Jim's CJ-5, Walter following behind in his unmarked FDLE car.

"That's Wendy's Lincoln," Jim said, giving Thurman Jr. a look. "Now what?"

They climbed out, waited for Walter to park, then the three of them walked into the office together.

Wendy and her daughter, Jennifer, were sitting across from Police Chief Goody and an officer Jim knew to be Billy Jordan. Both women looked up as they entered, Wendy jumping up at the sight of Jim and moving right to him.

"Jim...!" she said. "Thurman...!"

Wendy grabbed Jim's arm for support and hung onto him tightly. Jim was surprised, but pleasantly so. He put his hand over the woman's warm hand and instinctively put his arm protectively around her.

This did *not* go over well with Orville Goody.

"Mrs. Jamison, you sit right back down."

"What's going on, Chief?" Jim wanted to know.

He got a nasty look in return.

"Mr. Starke, do not interfere with police business!"

Which was when Walter made a decision, then stepped in. "And what police business is that?" he wanted to know. "Chief...?"

This went over even less well with Orville Goody.

He gave the FDLE officer a mean look, stood up and said, "This is local business, none of yours."

"Any police business in the State of Florida is my business," Walter corrected the man. "Let's hear it."

Instead of answering, I.C.'s police chief looked at Walter standing with Jim and Thurman Jr., only a short while ago there being no friendship lost among the three men.

To Walter, Orville Goody said, "You suddenly best friends with the main suspects in your FDLE officer's murder...?"

Walter gave him a look back.

"I got a new suspect, Chief," he said. "Locked back in your cell there—"

"Oh, well...about that." Orville Goody suddenly looked sheepish. "Seems we had a jail break, just the one prisoner, but he's gone, just lit out. I'll get an APB out on him right away."

And he gave Walter Hightower a knowing smirk.

"If you mean the Chief's brother Oliver," Wendy threw in, "he walked out the front door about five minutes after my daughter and I got here."

To which Orville Goody gave her a murderous look.

"Chief Goody, if that proves true," Walter told him, "I *will* be arresting you. And *I'll* put the BOLO on your brother, so don't bother."

He pulled out his cell phone to do exactly that.

* * *

Outside in the parking lot, Officer Ray drove up and got out, then saw something in Jim's old CJ-5 parked there that made him smile to himself.

He leaned into the vehicle as he passed by, picked up the object he'd seen, then kept going into the building.

* * *

When Officer Ray Lanyard walked in as if nothing in the world worth noting was going on, Walter had just finished putting out the BOLO on Oliver Goody and was closing up his cell phone.

He turned back to Chief Goody.

"Now, let's hear about this *local* crime involving these two women you're so much on top of..." he said with authority.

Orville Goody gestured toward Wendy, still standing next to and pretty much glued to Jim Starke.

"We got us a dead man at the I.C. Motel," he started. "Shot twice in the head, close range, Mrs. Wendy Jamison here and her daughter claiming self-defense."

"He tried to kill us!" Jennifer said.

Walter looked to each of the three of them.

"And, Chief, you don't believe them because...?"

As Orville Goody got into the details of the motel shooting with Walter, Jim and Thurman Jr. moved Wendy to the side so they wouldn't be overheard.

"What happened?" Jim wanted to know. "And don't worry, Thurman and I will keep an eye on you from now on."

Wendy smiled at that, then exhaled slowly.

"I'm taking evidence against my ex-husband to the Florida State Attorney's office on Monday. He sent two men to get it." She took a deep breath, looked to each of the men now apparently protecting her from *whatever*. "There was a shooting. I killed one and shot the other one."

Jim exchanged a quick look with Thurman Jr., then turned back to Wendy.

"You carry a gun?" he asked her.

"And where is he now?" Thurman Jr. asked. "The other one...?"

Wendy gestured vaguely.

"Out there," she said. "Somewhere. I shot him twice." She showed them on herself, where she'd hit him, "Right here. He's got to be hurting."

"Damn," Thurman Jr. said. "I'll bet he's pissed off."

Jim turned to where Chief Goody was still going back and forth with Walter Hightower.

"Chief, is Wendy under arrest...?"

"I'm still questioning her," the man insisted.

"I couldn't reach my lawyer," Wendy said.

Thurman Jr. volunteered, "My dad has a good one. We'll call him."

Jim gave a questioning look to Walter, who just shrugged. He turned back to Police Chief Orville Goody.

"Wendy and her daughter are going with us," he told the man, then motioned for Jennifer to stand up.

Chief Goody, enraged, stepped forward to stop them but Walter stepped in front of him. He stood eye-to-eye with the big man.

"Let's keep it civilized, Chief," he said easily. "Like the man said, arrest her or let her walk."

Orville Goody stood his ground a moment longer, then backed up.

"You people are going to regret this." he promised. "Seriously."

Jim told him, "If you need Wendy or her daughter for anything, they'll be staying at the Thurman place tonight."

And he and Thurman Jr. led Wendy and Jennifer out the front door without a look back.

Walter looked to both Officer Ray and Officer Jordan, shook his head with disgust, and headed back to the office they'd given him. No one said a word.

As soon as he was gone, Chief Goody looked to Ray, got a subtle nod that the deed he'd sent the man on was done.

Ex-I.C. Police Officer John Pasco was dead.

Chapter 49

When they all came out the front door of the Police Department, Wendy looked to her Lincoln, still sitting next to Jim's CJ-5.

"My car..." she said, uncertain what to do about it.

"Let's get it later," Jim suggested. "We'll just pull out your luggage."

Jennifer, knowing her own mother better than anyone alive and realizing she'd *never* go along with simply walking away from the damn ridiculous big car she loved so much, said, "Yeah, right."

And then was surprised when Wendy said, "Okay."

Jennifer gave her mother a look, then took a better look at Jim Starke, not certain that she liked what was going on there. The guy did not look particularly civilized, although *anyone* (after meeting her real family in the woods earlier today) would seem normal by comparison.

Of course, it really was the *other* character here, Thurman Jr., that did scare the young girl to death.

He looked like he could kill without a moment's hesitation or an ounce of thoughtful remorse. Jennifer planned to simply not talk to him and, in every way possible, to stay as far away as possible from that mean-looking guy.

* * *

As they crossed the intersection to get to the huge old Thurman house on the opposite corner, Jim and Thurman Jr. carrying their luggage, young Jennifer looked to the spooky three-story home with genuine trepidation.

It seemed to her to be only moments away from just falling down, probably waiting to collapse with them all inside.

She was also thinking, *Bats? Rats? Something worse?*

Thurman Jr., walking beside her, noticed her dubious look, because he said, "Don't worry, kid, it only looks haunted."

Which made her jump. His rough voice, so near.

"I didn't say anything," she said with a nervous half-laugh.

Jim was looking around the neighborhood as they crossed and when they reached the Thurman's front yard, he said to Wendy, "Your 'other guy' is sitting in an old Ford Taurus station wagon parked way back, down a side street." At her reaction, he said, "Don't look."

Jennifer was also starting to look around when, hearing Jim, she stopped and pretended to just walk on. "But that's him!" she said under her breath. "The old station wagon!"

"Let's go tell Chief Goody," Wendy said right away.

"We'll go have a talk with the man first," Jim told her.

Wendy stopped dead and looked to him with surprise.

"Jim, that man's psychotic. And extremely dangerous."

"We'll need him to testify against your ex-husband," he explained to her. "It's probably the only way."

"He'd never do that," she said. "He's a paid criminal—"

Jim and Thurman Jr. exchanged a quick look, but didn't respond.

Instead, they led Wendy and Jennifer up the stairs, across the wide front porch, and into the house.

Chapter 50

With the door closed to his temporary office at the I.C. Police department, Walter was on both his phone and his laptop computer as he talked, moving expertly through various law enforcement websites.

"So, Lieutenant, what've you got...?"

"No surprises on Police Chief Orville Goody or his idiot brother Oliver—going way back, lynching's, disappearances and every other form of racial intimidation." He sadly added, "But... nothing's ever stuck."

"Maybe it won't matter," Walter mused.

There was a long moment of silence. Then:

"Walter, if the chief of police there is involved in Elmore's death, I want him convicted, not dead. Is that clear?"

Ignoring the order, Walter said, "He's involved, all right." Then, changing the subject, "What about my two new redneck friends?"

"Surprise," the lieutenant said. "James M. Starke and Horace Thurman Jr., no arrests, no prison, not even a traffic ticket between them. We're checking military, credit, stuff like that, but so far they're upstanding citizens."

Walter shook his head, not believing it.

"These are two hardcore boys, Lieutenant, for real, like the kind you'd meet on death row," he said. "An I.C. police officer resigned rather than sign a complaint against them. Does that sound upstanding?"

"It doesn't. You figure they're in on it?"

Walter took a moment.

"I'm having my doubts," he admitted. "But they're damn dangerous. I saw hard-ass losers here, *really* hardcore, the kind normal people'd be afraid of, who wouldn't even look 'em in the eye—there's *something* there."

The Lieutenant sighed audibly through the phone.

"Okay, let me see what else I can find..."

"In a hurry. I'd appreciate it."

Chapter 51

Mr. Thurman Sr. had been surprisingly pleased to meet Wendy and Jennifer and was openly happy to share his home with them for the night. The shocking loss of his wife had staggered him, almost killed him, he thought, but he was very good at putting on a brave front.

He led them all up the back stairway to the second floor bedrooms.

Unlike the exterior of the spooky old house, the interior was surprisingly clean and in exceptional repair. In addition, the furniture and everything else within sight showed excellent taste and quality.

The Thurman's, Jennifer realized, had money. At least enough to nicely handle the upkeep on such a huge place.

On the stairs, Thurman Jr., Jennifer, Wendy and Jim followed Mr. Thurman up to see the bedroom the women would share.

Jennifer, badly frightened by the events that afternoon, didn't want to sleep on her own. That was a first, her mother knew.

"Have you talked to your sister?" Jim, at the rear with Wendy, asked.

"I tried," Wendy admitted. "Out at the trailers. But Pam's always mad at me, it seems. What's her problem, do you think?"

Jim shrugged, wasn't about to try answering that one.

"You dated her," she went on, giving him a look he couldn't quite read. "Starting when I moved away, right after high school..."

"Off and on, I guess."

"But you wouldn't date me," Wendy pointed out.

Jim said, "But you and I were together a lot..."

"But you wouldn't *date* me," the woman said. "And whenever I ask Pam about you, she gets all annoyed and obnoxious."

Jim stopped on the stairs, letting the rest of them get ahead.

"You asked Pam about me?" he said. "I didn't know that."

As soon as the two Thurman's and Jennifer disappeared around the corner at the top of the stairs, into the long hallway, Wendy moved directly in front of Jim on the stairway.

Almost pressing herself into him, she looked into his eyes.

As anyone in I.C. always knew, Wendy Jamison was not shy. With her looks, she never had to be.

"I wanted to date you," she informed him. "I thought about it a lot. All the time, in fact."

"You kissed me today. First time ever. Why couldn't you have done that back in high school...?"

Her look of surprise was genuine.

"You didn't want me to."

"I didn't...?"

That was probably true. Or at least, true enough, based on the way he'd acted around her. Like a good friend. A good friend without the slightest romantic interest in her. In other words, considering he was a boy with a *definite* romantic interest in her, a total idiot.

"I gave you enough chances," Wendy went on. "And I was, uh, with a lot of guys I didn't even like. You could have had me by just giving me a look. Or...pretty much anything."

Damn.

"I guess we were *both* idiots," he said.

Which was when Wendy Jamison gave him a look, then kissed him for real, a long sensuous kiss that pressed Jim against the wall, that almost knocked both of them down.

He found it easy to encircle her slim waist with his arms, to hold onto her tightly. And to barely believe it was finally happening.

"Wow," she breathed, as they separated. "I liked that."

"I didn't hate it." Jim studied her face as if just noticing it. Finally, after twenty-something years. He said, "God, I forgot how perfect your face really is. You look even better in real life than you do on TV."

"Jim...are you finally flirting with me?"

"Maybe."

She nodded then, and they began walking up the stairway again.

"So, all these years, you stayed in I.C.—*what* is your story?"

Jim shrugged.

"The usual. School, the Army, back home to live. Just that."

It was her turn to study *his* face.

There was something there, something she couldn't begin to define. She shook her head after a brief moment.

"Why don't I believe that...?"

Chapter 52

Walter Hightower, still at his desk behind a closed door at the I.C. Police Department, took out his ringing cell phone.

"Lieutenant..." he said.

"Your two new boyfriends," the man said. "The military had some things to say."

Walter nodded to himself.

"Dishonorable discharges? Military prison...?"

Lieutenant Scribner said, "Horace W. Thurman Jr., Staff Sergeant, heavy combat in the first Gulf War, many classified assignments, decorated multiple times, discharged with honor—the guy's a fucking war hero."

"I'll be damned. And Jim Starke...?"

"Dead opposite."

"I *knew* it."

"James Starke barely served," the Lieutenant went on. "No combat, no injuries, no distinctions. He's got a two-page folder."

Walter was suddenly confused.

"He didn't *do* anything...? What, he hid out? Went AWOL?"

"And no date of discharge."

"I don't get it."

"Walter, he's still active duty military."

"So he *is* a deserter..."

"Nope."

Now Walter was really confused.

"He's just sitting here in this craphole town..."

"Right, " the Lieutenant said. "Located two or so hours down from MacDill Air Force Base up in Tampa."

"Okay..."

"I came into FDLE directly out of Joint Military Intelligence," his superior said. "At MacDill AFB. I still got high-level friends there. Here's a clue: on Starke's folder, there's an ultraviolet stamp. Karma."

"Lieutenant, I don't know what you're saying. Like in India, karma?"

"It's an inside joke," he said. "For a department that technically doesn't exist, a pay-back unit that never was and never will be. As the most civilized nation in the world, we no long sanction invisible killers, not even for our worst enemies..."

It took a moment for the implications of all *that* to sink in.

"Are you fucking kidding me?"

"Walter, I'm forgetting what I just told you and I'm ordering you to do the same."

"Damn," Walter said.

But there was no one to hear it.

Lieutenant Scribner had already clicked off without another word.

Chapter 53

It was true, of course.

Jim Starke earned the green checks he received every month at his P.O. box up in Clewiston for certain dark skills rendered over the years, in unblinking service to his country.

Several times a year, he'd disappear for a few days and (surprise), no one in I.C. ever missed him or even wondered where he'd gone.

A decade and a half after multiple assignments in the Middle East, in Bosnia, Somalia, Afghanistan, Iran, Iraq and even South America, he was still technically active duty, although invisible. His membership, as it were, could not be proved by any official or existing paperwork.

Only by the absence of it. He had no discharge papers.

As Walter Hightower had so recently learned, Jim's was a specialty profession, in a specialty division appropriately nicknamed *Karma*, that did not allow for any form of retirement.

Not for the living, at least.

And, as mentioned, Interception City was conveniently located just 186 miles southeast of MacDill Air Force Base up in Tampa, home and headquarters to the Joint Military Intelligence Division, which oversaw covert military operations throughout the world, including projects requiring the invisible Jim Starke's specialty:

Sanctioned retribution.

These days, in truth, however, there were many of these assignments (handled entirely through a sense of duty and, eventually, sheer momentum) that Jim Starke had finally come to not remotely enjoy.

A lifetime of clandestine adventures under official government sanction (think: professional murder in the line of duty) eventually grew old.

Mostly, he was lonely.

Chapter 54

Wendy absently but carefully unpacked her suitcase, putting her personal toilet items on top of the antique dresser next to the window, while Jim stood just outside the door, talking in to her.

Her daughter, Jennifer, had decided to take her own room after all, once she saw the pleasant bedroom across the hall from her mother's. It was complete with a huge canopied bed, its own private bathroom and a huge claw-footed tub.

"Wendy, are you all right?" Jim suddenly asked.

He'd noticed that, for no apparent reason, she'd begun to silently cry as she stood there. It was obvious she was trying to hide her tears from Jim, but he moved into the room, then touched her arm.

"Wendy...?"

She exhaled, wiped at her eyes with a hand, then admitted, "I'm sorry. I've got another problem, one I'd discussed with Edna June on the phone. And now she's dead, so it complicates everything."

Before Jim could respond, Wendy went to the door and called, "Jennifer, are you okay over there?"

"Of course, Mother," the teen called back from across the hall. "I'm fine. And I love this room."

Wendy nodded, then carefully closed the door to her own bedroom. When she turned to Jim, she said, "I'm not certain how to begin—"

"What were you talking to Edna June about?" he asked.

"Her granddaughter."

Jim frowned.

"Edna June didn't have a granddaughter."

"Yes, she did," Wendy exhaled. "She just didn't know it for the last fourteen years. No one did."

Jim looked with shock to Jennifer's room.

"Your daughter...?"

"Edna June was furious I'd kept it from her."

Jim was still reeling.

"You and Thurman Jr...? He doesn't know?"

Wendy shook her head.

"I asked Edna June to let me tell him. She promised she'd wait just the one day, until I got here for the high school reunion." She shook her head sadly. "But now she's dead and she never even got to meet Jennifer—and Jennifer didn't get to meet her own grandmother."

And she began silently crying again, tears streaming down her perfect face.

"Leonard knew I was already pregnant," she haltingly got out. "He said it didn't matter to him...when we got married."

Jim nodded understanding.

"But *again*, you and Thurman Jr....?"

Wendy looked away, took out a tissue and wiped again at her eyes.

"Thurman and I ran into each other in Orlando years ago and got together for a drink," she said. "One thing led to another. By the time I knew I was pregnant, we were no longer speaking."

"Right."

"He's not an easy man to know."

"Really?"

She gave him a sharp look.

Jim looked out the window, saw Thurman Jr. in the yard below, clearing brush. Wendy joined him at the window, watched Thurman Jr. for several long moments. Jim could not imagine, though he tried, what the woman standing next to him was thinking.

"I was wild in high school," she said finally. "I knew they called me the school whore and a lot of other names, but, like you, Thurman was my best friend and I stupidly thought..."

She turned away.

"Anyway, it was stupid," she said. "And Jennifer's going to hate me when she learns the truth."

She looked to Jim then, looking as helpless as he'd ever seen her—which was *never*—and he suddenly put his arms out and pulled her close, hugging her in a strong, mostly platonic embrace.

He exhaled slowly.

"Okay, let's just try to handle it," he told her. "We'll have figure it out."

Chapter 55

In the big front office at Oliver Goody's junkyard, Police Chief Orville Goody and Officer Ray were addressing a ragtag group made up of supposed jail-escapee Oliver Goody, his hefty lunkhead of a son Lukas, employee Danny Bird, Alligator Pit-owner Big Jeff Welsher and Sherman Anderson, whose broken and smashed nose had gauze and bandages taped across it.

Orville Goody announced, "Jim Starke and Thurman Jr. have harmed, or maybe killed, one of my men, Officer John Pasco."

He paused for effect.

"They attacked him once, no telling what's happened to the man. He's not around, no more, that we can tell—"

"What about that black cop?" Oliver wanted to know

Officer Ray gave him a smirk.

"He's throwing his weight around," Ray said. "Being the big man among the white natives, I guess..."

"What are you suggesting, Chief...?" Sherman Anderson wanted to know.

Gingerly touching at his nose, he was hoping it'd be something bad, something *really* bad, that the police chief was planning, especially as it pertained to Jim Starke. He desperately wanted to get even with the man but wasn't exactly certain how to go about it.

The Chief held up his hand for attention.

"Men, this wouldn't be the first time a group of lawful citizens worked behind the scenes to keep our community safe." And, after again pausing for effect, "There ain't much of a real Klan left, even in these parts, but I'm saying we step up..."

"But, Chief, that black man's a cop," Big Jeff pointed out.

Orville Goody had anticipated that response.

"Jeff, there's a big difference between a killing and a disappearance," he said, which after some thoughtful pondering, got general nods of approval. "We live in the middle of a gigantically huge swamp, after all..."

His brother Oliver then said, "Orville, taking down Jim Starke or Thurman Jr. could be real tricky. Them are, uh, two dangerous boys..."

Chief Goody shook his head at the thought, then gave Officer Ray a knowing glance.

"No man's a further threat once he's dead...." was what he then said.

And the others finally had to nod, and smile, at the thought. They all recognized the absolute truth when they heard it.

* * *

Still sitting far enough back on a side street to not be noticed by most, Tommy Luercher in the Ford Taurus station wagon continued to watch the Interception City Police Department and the Thurman house across the intersection.

He'd seen Judge Leonard Johnson's two bitches of a wife and daughter cross over with the two large rednecks, all of them disappearing into the decrepit old house, and he right then decided he wasn't in that great of shape, not to take on two men he knew nothing about.

Better, he thought, to wait until the wife came back out on her own, possibly to cross over to the parking lot where she'd left her big Lincoln.

He'd kill her then, just drive up and shoot her the first moment he saw her, then drive away and wait outside of town until it was time to meet the judge with his money at the local high school reunion.

Of course, he blamed Judge Leonard Johnson for the entire mess, including the death of his cousin, Eugene. The fucking asshole could have told them the woman was dangerous. Highly dangerous.

Or at least that she carried a fucking gun.

For that lack of information, Tommy would shoot the Judge point blank in the face as soon as he had the money in his hands.

That would be justice, after all.

In any case, Tommy was in great pain still.

The bleeding seemed to have stopped, especially after he stuffed two of Eugene's extra tee-shirts against the wounds and then put his belt tightly around himself to keep them in place.

The only problem, as he saw it, was that he was so damn sleepy.

And he did not want to miss his shot at Wendy when she finally came back outside and crossed the street.

Chapter 56

Jim and Wendy were still watching Thurman Jr. down in the yard below.

Typical of the big man, he continued working at clearing away brush even though his mother had been found dead, murdered, in fact, that very morning. Keeping his mind occupied, keeping himself occupied, even in times of great stress or pain, was his nature.

Jim knew him that well.

He asked Wendy, "Do you want me to go with you when you tell him...?"

She shook her head.

"I'll be fine."

She then took a breath, steadied herself and headed out the door to explain the mistake she'd made (not telling the man was the main one) so many years ago. Fourteen and eleven months, to be exact.

He'd not be happy about it, that was for sure.

Jim stayed at the window, watching.

He reacted without turning to a slight noise behind him, wasn't surprised when Jennifer walked up to the window and stood beside him.

"Where'd my mom go?" she asked.

They both watched as Wendy walked out in the yard to Thurman Jr., then stopped to talk to him.

Jennifer said to Jim, "People seem really afraid of your big friend, like he's so dangerous. Or a criminal. Is he?"

Jim looked to the girl.

"Is he what—dangerous or a criminal?"

"Both. Either."

Out in the yard below, they saw Wendy say something to Thurman Jr. that caused him to suddenly look up to the window. He stared hard at Jim and Jennifer. The girl immediately stepped back.

"Yikes!" she said. "See...even I'm scared of him."

Jim turned and studied her a long moment, the daughter of Wendy Jamison and Horace Thurman Jr., a combination that was somehow completely shocking to him. That she was probably one tough kid already, and would grow up to be even tougher, far, far tougher, no doubt, although absolutely beautiful as well, would turn out to be no surprise.

"Thurman's no criminal," he finally said. "And you have no reason to ever be afraid of him."

She nodded slowly, not completely believing him.

"But he *is* dangerous..." she said. "Anyone can tell."

Jim didn't respond.

She went on, "I know my mom really appreciated your help at the police station earlier. We both did. So...were you my mom's boyfriend way back in high school or something?"

Jim shook his head.

"Just a close friend," he told her. "Only a friend."

"Uh huh,' she nodded, and Wendy's daughter seemed to accept it. "So what was my mother like?"

Jim thought about it.

"For one, she was the best-looking girl in school..."

Jennifer just rolled her eyes—it was completely old news to her. She was *also*, in fact, considered the best-looking girl in her own school, a feat she cared little about, mostly because she'd done nothing to attain it.

"Was she one of the good kids or one of the bad kids?"

Jim gave her a half-smile at the thought.

"I guess we were all...the bad kids."

Jennifer smiled back.

"Troublemakers."

"Something like that," he admitted. He sighed. "Let's go on down..."

* * *

Jim and Jennifer walked down the back stairs and discovered Wendy and Thurman Jr. in a conversation with Mr. Thurman Sr. at the large porcelain kitchen table. The table-group stopped talking abruptly when they walked in.

Wendy turned to Jennifer, as did the Thurman's, who then stared at the teen girl as if studying her face.

"What?" Jennifer asked. "Am I in trouble or something?"

"Not at all, dear," Mr. Thurman told her warmly.

Thurman Jr. said, "My God, you look exactly like your mother."

Jennifer exhaled with a little shake of her head. That was not a surprise to her, since she'd been hearing it all her life. It was good news, of course but still—she found it vaguely irritating as well.

"Okay, what's going on?"

Jim then said, "Wendy, give me your keys and I'll go over to get your car from the police station."

"I'll go with you," Jennifer volunteered.

Surprising them all, including Jim.

"No, you're not," Wendy told her daughter. "We need to talk..."

Jennifer gave her a look, then looked to the others.

She crossed her slender arms in front of her, stood as if not wanting to hear *whatever* this was all about. God!

It was obviously going to be something *weird*.

"Now what...?"

Chapter 57

Jim walked casually across the intersection, ignoring the hanging stoplight because there were only a few cars around and they were mostly parked, only the occasional vehicle driving through.

He never looked over to the old Ford Taurus station wagon sitting far back on a side street, but he kept it in his peripheral vision in case the man inside decided to climb out and approach him. When he reached the police station's asphalt parking lot, Jim went to Wendy's Lincoln, parked next to his own CJ-5.

He slid in behind the wheel of Wendy's car, looked around, then started it and pulled the car across the street. He drove around the side of the Thurman home, then parked it out of sight in the back.

Several minutes later, he had crossed through backyards and swampy vacant fields until he saw the shape of the man who'd attacked Wendy and

Jennifer sitting behind the wheel of the old Ford station wagon.

Jim moved silently up to it from behind.

He saw the muscular man was sitting with his head back against the headrest, the driver's window down. The car wasn't running, the heat within the vehicle easily over a hundred degrees at that time of day.

Flicking open a black 13" switchblade knife as he moved to the open car window, Jim swiftly put the blade against the man's throat, realized instantly the paid killer was dead. He'd clearly bled out, the seat covered with a huge stain of his slowly-blackening blood.

Jim took a moment to take the man's cell phone and wallet, then saw Wendy's burgundy leather briefcase on the back seat.

* * *

Jim walked back to the house with Wendy's briefcase, discovered Jennifer sitting alone on the wide front porch in a lawn chair. The girl quickly looked away, at the same time wiping at her eyes.

"Hey," Jim said. "You okay?"

The girl gave him an accusing look.

"Do you know who my real dad is?"

Jim had to nod.

"I just found out, too," he admitted. "He's a good man."

Jennifer seemed paralyzed with shock.

"He's too scary," she breathed.

"He's one of the good guys." Jim assured her. "You'll see."

The blonde teen studied Jim doubtfully, would clearly require more than just words from Thurman Jr.'s best friend to believe it.

"I'm not related to the family I grew up with," she said finally, looking away. "My father, I mean. It's like I was...adopted. And I just met my mom's family today. Except for her sister, my Aunt Pam, I guess, they're all so...awful."

Jim didn't react, but he couldn't disagree with her assessment. Wendy and Pam were the only two good apples in the bunch, the rest of the Jamison's a pack of wild jackals living in the deep swamp.

Jennifer said, "My mother made me think we were coming here for her stupid reunion." She went silent, thoughtful, and then, suddenly panicked, "My God, are we *moving* down here...?!"

And she started crying.

"Only your mom can answer that," Jim told her. "But I seriously doubt it."

At that, Jennifer brightened slightly and sniffled, "Really? Oh, God, I hope you're right. I totally *hate* it down here!" And then noticing, "You got my mom's briefcase back!"

Jim held it up for her to see.

"It was easy enough," he said.

Jennifer looked to him.

"Is he...dead?"

Meaning the terrible man who'd taken it.

Jim silently nodded just as the screen door opened and Wendy and Thurman Jr. walked out onto the porch. At the sight of them, Jennifer stiffened, then got up and stalked back into the house.

They could all hear her stomping up the front stairs to her room.

"God, I knew this wouldn't be easy," Wendy said. "Thurman..."

But Thurman Jr. was looking to his lifelong friend.

"Jim-boy..." he said.

Jim gave him a look back.

"Yeah, we got things to talk about," he said. "Later." He held up the briefcase. "The man in the car is dead. I went out to see him, got this back." And at Wendy's look, "I didn't kill him. He bled out."

He showed them Tom Luercher's wallet and cell phone, then brought up 'calls dialed' on the phone, held it up for Wendy to see. She steadied his hand with her own, but he didn't react to her touch.

He was still trying to get his mind around the entire Wendy/Thurman Jr. thing.

"The last call was to Leonard's cell phone," she told them both.

Jim hit the button for 'speaker' and the number. They all listened to it ring once and then again before:

"Goddamn it, I said I'd be at that fucking reunion at 8:00 tonight," a man's voice came through loud and clear, annoyed to say the least. "I'm driving down there right now. Luercher...?"

Wendy nodded to them: it was Leonard.

Jim hung up, handed her the phone.

"Hang onto this," he told her. "The call log's evidence."

Wendy nodded, taking the phone and putting it into her briefcase, but she was studying him, subtly yet carefully.

He looked away, pretended not to notice her sudden concern.

He realized it was probably obvious to her that something was different, that their relationship, or lack of one, had been permanently altered (and probably not in a good way) by her admission about Thurman Jr. being the father of her teenage daughter.

Chapter 58

Oliver Goody was making coffee over a small campfire in front of a falling-down tin-roof shack in the swamp, the front door barely hanging on. Most of the windows were broken out, the roof sagging badly in the middle.

It was the old Bartow place, the last owner an aged bootlegger who'd died years earlier.

Leaning against the tilted porch, within easy reach, were two automatic shotguns and a Chinese AK-47, just in case. Oliver, though supposedly on the run from the law, was in a remarkably good mood.

Truth be told, his junkyard business had gotten almost intolerably boring over the years and he was pleased to be away from it for a while. His son Lukas could handle the business until Orville Goody straightened out the mess they'd all found themselves in, mostly due to that goddamn black Corvette sports car.

He should've buried that vehicle in the swamp the second he laid eyes on it. Hanging onto it, even for the short time he'd had it, was stupid, stupid, stupid.

A sudden rustling in the tropical growth surrounding the small clearing made him drop the coffee pot and reach for a shotgun. He had it in his hands extremely fast and trained it directly on a skinny man who suddenly appeared through the thick underbrush.

"Whoa, partner..." the man said, rattled as well. He'd been carrying an old bolt-action Springfield rifle but quickly dropped it and raised his hands. "Din't mean to startle you or nothing—I'm like you, poaching 'gators."

Oliver studied him, thought he might recognize the man, then exhaled and lowered the shotgun.

It was merely that imbecile Delmar Spinks, a poacher like he'd said, harmless in every way unless you happened to be an alligator or one of the Everglade National Park's thirty-six threatened or protected species including the Florida panther, the rare American crocodile or a West Indian manatee.

The man would kill and eat any damn thing.

"Sit right down there in the dirt, Delmar," Oliver told him. "And keep your hands where I can see 'em...we need to talk."

Chapter 59

With Jim Starke in the lead, he and Wendy and Thurman Jr. walked into the I.C. Police Department like they owned the place.

Walter was standing at the FAX machine with a handful of pages in his hand, Officer Billy Jordan seated at the front desk. Jordan gave them all a nervous glance, then called back over his shoulder, "Chief, you got visitors..."

Which brought Police Chief Orville Goody right out.

Jim told him, "The other shooter Wendy told you about is sitting dead in his car, a Ford Taurus station wagon, exactly like she said, back along 2nd Avenue, near Russell Hart's place."

The Chief nodded.

"That so...? You kill him?"

"Not me," Jim said. "Looks like he bled to death."

"We'll see. You touch anything? Take anything?"

Jim shook his head.

"Not me."

"We'll check it out."

But Chief Goody made no move, instead pointedly waited for the three of them to simply leave his front office. Wendy gave the man a disgusted look, realized they'd get no further help from the overweight police chief of her own hometown.

Walter smiled, motioned for the three of them.

"Come on back," he said with an exaggerated drawl. "Let's set a spell."

"Right," Jim said.

Inside his office, Walter shut the door behind them, then sat on the front of his desk, arms crossed. He nodded to them politely, studied them as he might a strange mix of
plant life. Or aliens.

The three of them remained standing.

To Jim and Thurman Jr. he said, "You two are a couple of real interesting good old boys, I got to admit. Not what I expected." To Wendy, he added, "And *you,* I know from TV up in Orlando, but what you're doing down here, I got no idea..."

Wendy suddenly looked uncomfortable.

"My high school reunion," she finally said, close enough, really. "I'm originally from down here."

"My condolences."

He waited, but none of the three people standing before him volunteered anything further, so Walter said:

"I need to get something straight. My older brother Elmore came down here on the way to the Keys to meet a young white woman he found on the Internet." He paused at the thought of it, but went on, "And he ends up dead with an *older* white woman in a burned-up SUV with 4 bullet holes in him."

And he waited again.

This time, Jim said, "I'm certain Edna June didn't even know your brother. And I'm betting she never met *anyone* through the Internet."

"Never," Thurman Jr. threw in. "She didn't like computers."

Walter thought it over.

"But she ended up in her SUV with Elmore."

All of them then thought that one over.

"And his car ended up out at Oliver Goody's junkyard," Jim said.

Thurman Jr. added, "Which the fat-assed fuck denied knowing anything about—while we were standing there *looking* at the goddamn thing!"

"Yes, he did..." Walter agreed.

"We need to find Oliver Goody," Jim said. "And have a painful talk with him. Alone. Same with ex-police officer John Pasco."

Walter gave him a sharp look.

"I hope you're not talking about breaking the law," he said. And when he got no answer, "But you're right; Officer Pasco knows *something* about all this..." And then, remembering, "Elmore said he was meeting a '...young hot-assed little slut, married but bored,' down here in Interception City proper."

Jim and Thurman Jr. both nodded.

"We've got some desperately bored young things around," Thurman Jr. agreed. "Married or not, no question."

Wendy said, "Everyone will mostly be at the reunion tonight—it's all-grades, so young and old and everything in-between..."

Walter looked to the three of them, thoughtful again.

"Maybe I should bring in an entire SWAT team, grab John Pasco to start, shake up the place..."

"You won't get any fast answers that way," Jim disagreed.

"Okay, then I need to be at that reunion," Walter continued. "If I had some locals to show me around..."

Jim looked to him.

"Are you asking us out on a date?"

"Funny," Walter said, smiling without humor. He pushed away from his desk. "You redneck crackers are seeming funnier to me by the minute..."

Chapter 60

Three hours later at the Thurman home, the remains of dinner were still on the table while Jennifer and Mr. Thurman Sr. sat alone, eating homemade apple pie with French vanilla ice cream.

Jennifer liked the older man, more than kindly and seemingly very intelligent, but she was still trying to grasp, emotionally as well as intellectually, that the man was her actual grandfather.

It seemed impossible, yet at the same time, true enough.

They were blood, she and this family that basically lived in the absolute middle of nowhere, in a swampy jungle, in fact, as near-savages (as far as she was concerned) as it was possible to be.

"You must realize, young lady," the older man was saying to her, causing her to look up from her plate, "I'm as shocked as you are, as is my son.

We had no idea." He took a steadying breath. "And my poor wife, your grandmother..."

But his voice caught and he looked away, unable to go on.

"It's like I'm in a dream," the girl said. "Everything I thought I knew, is wrong. And my dad, my was-real dad, is *not* my dad at all. And is trying to kill my mom!"

Mr. Thurman Sr. shook his head.

"I've had my share of shocks as well."

Jennifer looked to him, realized the pain he must be feeling.

"I'm really sorry," she said quietly. "I'm thinking only of me and you've lost your wife. I really am sorry."

The older man looked to her, nodded his thanks.

She could suddenly hear Jim Starke and Thurman Jr. coming down the back stairs and they both appeared in the kitchen a moment later, each dressed in casual slacks, tropical shirts and sport coats.

She was surprised at how nicely they cleaned up. Shocked was more like it.

"Jennifer..." Thurman Jr. started, a little awkwardly, it seemed. "How are you doing?"

She actually tried a smile.

"You look very nice," she said. "You both do,"

Which clearly surprised the big man she now knew to be her real father.

"Thanks."

A moment later, Wendy walked in from the front room wearing a clingy lightweight little black dress that radiated the heat of her perfect body. She was gorgeous and, apparently, knew it.

Jim could only stare at her without speaking, realizing once again that, even after all the years since he'd last seen her, the woman was still so stunningly beautiful she was almost electric.

"Do I look okay?" Wendy asked, doing a half-turn for them.

"Mother..." Jennifer shook her head, openly annoyed (as usual) with their beauty. "Why do you even have to ask?"

But Thurman Jr. said, "You're going to drive every man there crazy."

"Right," was all Jim said.

And Wendy, showing just the merest hint of concern at Jim's lack of praise, said simply, "Good,"

Chapter 61

The Interception City High School was a large one-story block building with a tall two-story gymnasium at one end, surrounded (no surprise) by seemingly endless tropical jungle and swamp.

In the huge parking lot were many older cars, pick-up trucks and SUV's, taking up nearly all the spaces. The all-grades I.C. high school reunion looked to be a real success, thought Wendy, as they pulled into the parking area and drove to the rear of the lot to find a space.

Thurman Jr. was driving her big Lincoln, Wendy beside him.

Walter's unmarked car pulled in a moment later, following them, Jim Starke in the passenger seat.

All four of them got out, looked over at the school itself.

Jim asked, "Remember much about this place, Wendy?"

She gave him an uncertain look.

"All of a sudden I do," she said. "And I'm not so sure I want to go in."

"It'll be fine," Thurman Jr. assured her. "If anybody gets out of line..."

She turned to him with a severe look.

"Thurman, I appreciate your concern, but I can take care of myself—"

"I think the lady has proven that," Walter cut in. "Shall we...?"

And he gestured toward the open double-doors where everyone seemed to be entering the building. Wendy turned to him.

"Thank you, Officer Hightower," she told him. "And guys, please don't start a big fight in there..."

"Us...?" Jim said, but then, "No problem. Okay, then..."

And they headed for the gym.

* * *

Parked in front of John Pasco's modest home, blue lightbars still flashing, were all three I.C. PD squad cars, the police chief's unmarked car and an ambulance. The few neighbors nearby were trying to see what was going on, but were held back by two I.C. police officers, called in off-shift, stiffly standing guard at the farthest perimeter.

Inside the home, the smell of gunpowder and blood was still more than evident.

Police Chief Orville Goody, Officer Ray, Officer Billy Jordan and Officer Carl Ledbetter stood by silently while Dr. Denton examined John Pasco's body. Behind them, already attended to by the County Coroner, Myra's body was being put onto a gurney by the two ambulance attendants.

Chief Goody looked down to what was left of Pasco.

"So those two rough boys managed to kill John after all," he intoned, sadly, as if to himself, and then turned to his officers. "Pasco wouldn't sign a complaint against 'em, Jim Starke and Horace Thurman Jr., which I strongly recommended," he said, then decided to take the opportunity: "Goddamn it to hell, I tell you boys to do something, I usually got a good goddamn reason for it."

They all nodded numbly, still shocked at seeing one of their very own dead right before their eyes.

"Chief, you did everything you could," Officer Ray added. "Everything."

The police chief nodded.

"He was a good man—them boys'll pay."

* * *

A huge brightly-colored paper banner above the doorway of the gymnasium lobby proclaimed: *I.C. High School All-Grades Reunion!*

From inside, loud rockabilly music was blaring.

As Jim, Walter, Thurman Jr. and Wendy stood at the reception table before going in, it was obvious their arrival had badly flustered the alumni who was sitting behind it, a somewhat chunky red-faced woman who, tight-lipped and pinchy-faced, could not seem to get a single word out.

All of them turned to meet the school principal when he walked up.

He was robust man in his late-30's, with thinning hair and black-framed glasses, who took a moment to glance at their name tags.

Or lack of one.

Wendy's pre-printed tag named her as WENDY JAMISON-JOHNSON, although she'd used a pen to cross out the Johnson part. Walter Hightower had simply picked up a blank one for guests and filled in *A Friend* with the same pen. Neither Jim nor Thurman Jr. had bothered with the formality.

Everyone in the entire county of Banyon knew who they were, anyway.

The principal smiled thinly, hesitated, then chose to offer Walter his hand.

"And welcome..." he said, when Walter gave his hand a quick shake and released it. "I'm Mr. James Potter, the principal here. And you are...?"

"Like it says—a friend."

This seemed to cause Mr. Potter some inner concern, but he gamely went on.

"Well...you are welcome, then...friend," he said. He turned to Thurman Jr., exhaled sadly. Sincerely. "Horace, we are shocked and saddened by your loss. And ours. Your mother...well, what can I say...will be greatly missed,"

Thurman Jr. tightly nodded his appreciation for the genuine sentiment, then looked away.

Mr. Potter gestured grandly for them all to enter the reunion.

"Please enjoy yourselves," he added.

Inside the gym, they discovered themselves in the middle of crepe-paper streamers, low lighting, many round cafeteria tables with paper tablecloths, most of them filled with the variously-aged alumni, and a youngish DJ on the raised platform at the front of the room that served as a stage.

"More people than I expected," Jim murmured.

An open bar stood along one wall, a long buffet table set up with hot food coming out, and three middle-aged couples were dancing to a *Stray Cats* tune from the 1980's, *Rock This Town*.

Everyone in the place looked up at their entrance.

"I don't recognize many of them," Wendy said, seeming relieved. But then, "Oh, God, there's one I do. Rusty Warren, looks like he married one of the Baxter girls. Let's go this way..."

Leading them away from Rusty's table.

Yet Jim saw the man staring at them, was certain he heard Rusty give a sharp yelp in pain, no doubt from Betsy Baxter's hard pinch at her husband's eyes resting on the gorgeous Wendy Jamison for a just moment too long.

"There's Pam and my cousin Sherman," Wendy said.

"Perfect," was Jim's response, but he followed her.

She stopped, looked to him.

"I need to say 'hi' since we're here," she said. "You don't want to sit with them do you...Jim?"

Meaning: with my annoying sister who you used to date?

"Well..."

But Thurman Jr. took the opportunity to interject, "Why not? We're looking for fun, right?"

Jim gave him a dirty look, but they all crossed the floor, nodding to a few people as they did so, yet getting only a nervous smile or two in return. Walter, trailing at the rear, had as yet not uttered a single word since entering the room.

There wasn't a single other black face in the place.

Pam Jamison and Sherman Anderson, both wearing printed name tags proclaiming them as such, were sitting alone at a round table big enough for six people. Neither of them looked happy to see Wendy, Jim or Thurman Jr., especially with Sherman's nose still bandaged up.

As for Walter, Sherman gave him a look of definite disapproval. In return Walter gave him a bright smile, pulled out a chair across from the man without being asked, then stood with his hand on the back of it and waited for the fun.

He was actually beginning to greatly enjoying giving all these redneck *assholes* a hard time.

"Hello again, Pam," Wendy said.

She seen the woman earlier that day out at the family's private trailer park in the deep woods, yet had had virtually no real conversation with her.

She looked to Anderson, who was already beginning to openly sulk at their arrival.

"Sherman..."

Pam nodded with a forced smile, looked to Jim but then looked away. As they all sat down, Thurman Jr. dropped into the seat next to Sherman Anderson.

"Hey, Anderson," the man with the straight-razor scar said to the man with the bandaged nose. "Stick that in where it didn't belong?"

Sherman scowled, but didn't look directly to the man confronting him.

"Ask your friend, Jimbo there—he sucker-punched me when I wasn't looking." He gestured towards Walter. "This colored man the big bad cop from the big bad city everybody's talking about...?"

Walter gave him another smile.

"I'm big and I'm bad and I *am* a cop," he admitted. "But you got something to say, say it. Boy."

Which is when Jim decided to intervene.

"Guys, it's a party, remember?"

Anderson scowled again, but apparently decided not to pursue it. Walter merely smiled again and looked around. Wendy, sitting next to her sister, tried to talk to Pam but wasn't having much luck.

Finally, clearly exasperated, Wendy turned to Jim.

"Can we go over and get a drink?" she asked.

Jim looked to the bar, then nodded.

"Yeah," he agreed. "And let's mingle."

Walter said, "Mingle?"

He shook his head with the first real laugh he'd had since arriving in this godforsaken shithole called Interception City early that morning.

"White boys—mingling."

Chapter 62

While the festivities were going on strong at the high school, Virginia Lanyard, still in just her underpants, tried using the metal edge of the handcuffs holding her to the bed to cut through the thick wooden post of the headboard.

"Son of a bitch...!" she rasped.

Her tear-streaked young face was twisted into a snarl, her eye swelling and blackening even further from the punch she'd taken from Officer Ray. The crotch of her panties were still soaked from when she'd peed on herself over an hour earlier.

She'd seen no reason to hold it, no reason to add to her discomfort, in the single-wide trailer she planned on never setting foot in again.

If she lived.

The sharp edge of the handcuffs barely scratched the post, causing her to finally give up and sag against the bed, her small hand and slender arm held upright in an awkward pose.

Mostly, she was terrified at the thought of her clearly insane husband coming home and deciding to simply kill her.

* * *

Outside of the Interception City High School, all three I.C. PD squad cars quietly pulled up and stopped at the curb.

Officers Billy Jordan, Carl Ledbetter and four other full-time and part-time policemen got out, all of them loaded down with heavy-duty weapons. They stood in place, waiting for Chief Orville Goody's car to arrive.

As Ray Lanyard pulled the chief's car to the curb and stopped, he said to his superior officer and father-in-law, "I don't know, Chief—we got 'em in jail, might be hard to, you know, get to 'em..."

Orville Goody gave him a dismissive wave.

"They won't live through the night."

Inside the I.C. High School gymnasium-turned-party-scene, Jim stood with Wendy and Walter at the bar, all with soft drinks.

Thurman Jr. stood slightly apart, talking to a skinny man wearing a Jeff Gordon NASCAR tee-shirt.

Jim quietly asked Wendy, "So, how are you and Thurman getting along?"

"He was surprised, of course," she said. "And after the stunt Leonard pulled, Jennifer wasn't as upset as I expected—"

Jim nodded understanding.

"When your supposed-father sends contract killers to visit, you're gonna have second thoughts about the man..."

Walter stepped closer, asked, "Any sight of ex-officer Pasco yet?"

Which was when Thurman Jr. put his arm over the shoulder of the skinny man in the NASCAR tee-shirt and turned him to face the group; it was the skinny man who ran into Oliver Goody in the swamp.

"I was asking my old friend Delmar here about my other good old buddy Oliver Goody, who I didn't see here tonight," Thurman Jr. said.

He encouraged the skinny man with a little squeeze of his arm, an action which further terrified Delmar at being in the dangerous man's grip. Delmar looked to each of them with uncertainty.

"Tell 'em, Delmar..."

"It weren't no big deal," the man started. "I was out near the old Bartow place in the swamp and it looked like Oliver was living there..."

"And...?" Thurman Jr. prodded.

"And he pulled a shotgun on me. Like I said, it weren't no big deal. He didn't shoot or nothing."

Thurman Jr. finally unhanded the man.

"Thanks, Delmar," he said. "Come on by the store Monday, I'll fix you up with some free stuff."

Which surprised the skinny man greatly.

"Why, *thanks*, Thurman..."

Which was exactly when the lights abruptly were turned all the way up and the music suddenly stopped in mid-song with a raw scratchy rasp.

Jim looked over, saw Officer Ray, Officer Jordan, Officer Ledbetter and three other I.C. policemen that he sort of recognized walk into the place, heavy weapons out and pointed in their direction.

On the stage, suddenly standing with a microphone in his hand next to the DJ, was I.C. Police Chief Orville Goody.

"Stay calm," the Chief announced. "We got us a *situation* here."

Jim looked to Thurman Jr. and Walter, then turned to Wendy and told her in no uncertain terms, "Whatever happens, do *not* get in this..."

But, of course, Wendy was already half-way across the gym floor before he finished, angrily heading directly to Chief Orville Goody, who'd already stepped down off the stage and was heading right at them.

Chapter 63

As Jim, Thurman Jr. and Walter Hightower calmly stood waiting for the gathering storm of I.C. police officers to come to them, Chief Orville Goody was followed across the floor by Wendy, yelling at him every step of the way.

Right behind the Chief and Wendy were Officers Ray and Billy Jordan, the other I.C. officers holding back the crowd.

"Jim Starke and Horace Thurman Jr.," Orville Goody announced, loudly, reaching them with Wendy still at his heels. "You are under arrest for the murder of I.C. Police Officer John Pasco and an as-yet-unidentified colored woman who was also living at the premises."

Walter could only shake his head.

"Chief Goody, what the hell are you doing?"

But the Chief ignored him and said, "Officer Lanyard, cuff 'em, pat 'em down and read 'em their rights."

Jim and Thurman Jr. stood unresisting and silent as Officers Ray and Billy Jordan carefully handcuffed their hands behind their backs, Ray using the black alloy cuffs he'd had to special order.

At the same time, Chief Goody took out a clear plastic evidence bag with Jim's sunglasses in it. Officer Ray couldn't resist smiling to himself.

Jim gave him a look, but said nothing.

"Chief...?" Walter said.

"Officer Hightower, I recognized these at the scene of the crime," the Chief said smugly. "They belong to Mr. Jim Starke, as fingerprints—I am absolutely certain—will soon verify."

He gestured impatiently to Officer Ray.

"Go on..."

Officer Ray first patted down Thurman Jr. with a clearly nervous touch, not meeting the larger man's gaze, then turned to search Jim as Wendy stepped directly in front of Chief Goody.

"I was with Jim and Thurman Jr. all afternoon," she told him. "So they couldn't have done it—"

The Chief merely nodded that he'd heard her.

"We'll see," he allowed. "But I don't consider you a credible witness." And, loud enough for everyone else to hear, he added, "You are currently the subject of a murder investigation in your own right..."

"Goddamn it, Chief Goody," she said. "You're being impossible."

In the background, they all heard Officer Ray murmur, "Jeeze oh peeze!"

They all turned to see what had caught his sudden attention, saw him holding Jim's H&K .45, his 9mm Glock 17 and the 13" black switchblade in his hands, all lifted from Jim's sports coat and pockets.

"Starke's armed to the damn teeth!"

Jim merely shrugged, watched as Officer Ray Lanyard put the big switchblade into his own pants pocket, held the two guns in both hands.

Thurman Jr. said to his friend, with disgust, "Damn, that's all the better you could hide a second gun?"

It was time for Walter to step up.

"I was also with these men this afternoon," he said.

Chief Orville Goody gave him a long look.

"Were you with 'em *all* afternoon?" the Chief wanted to know. "Every second...?"

Walter had to think about it a moment, then admitted, "No—but I'm certain they had nothing to do with your officer's death."

The Chief turned to his slack-jawed oaf of a son-in-law and said, "Officer Lanyard, move 'em both along..."

Walter gave Orville Goody a look of purest disgust. And total mistrust.

"Chief, I'm accompanying these men to your jail," he told the man. "I'm well aware of the unsolved homicides of men in your care over the years."

In his defense, Chief Goody said, "None of those were white men. But you do what you think best."

"That I will."

Chapter 64

Outside of the I.C. High School gymnasium, the entire reunion crowd followed as Jim Starke and Horace Thurman Jr. were walked out in handcuffs.

Police Chief Goody and Officer Ray, carrying Jim's two guns in one hand, led the way, Officers Carl Ledbetter (carrying a shotgun still) and Billy Jordan (with a full-auto M16) at the rear.

Unkown to any of them, Wendy's husband Federal Judge Leonard Johnson was sitting in his Lincoln at the back of the parking lot, having just arrived and trying without much luck to see what the hell all the excitement was.

He had a briefcase full of money ($25,000 from Wendy's cable TV show checking account) next to him on the passenger seat. All the police cars sitting up there were beginning to make him nervous.

He had no idea whether his wife was alive or finally dead, not knowing whether his paid killer had ever caught up with her, but he wondered if that was possibly *why* the local authorities were in such concentrated attendance.

For all he know, or hoped, Wendy's dead body might be the center of attention somewhere up there, murdered by crazy Tommy Luercher as she headed into the reunion.

And hope, hope, hope, maybe that psychopath Luercher himself had been gunned down by all those cops when he tried to get away.

The judge smiled to himself.

Wouldn't *that* be a nice scenario?

* * *

Two of the I.C. police cars pulled away from the curb in front of the school, one of them playfully hitting the lights and siren for just a quick moment as they left, each car carrying the officers who weren't transporting Jim and Thurman Jr. to the two cells at the downtown police department.

That was a job that'd be handled personally by the Chief and Officer Ray.

Wendy, so angry she was shaking and could barely catch her breath, was still berating Orville Goody.

"Damn it, Chief, you're wrong! They didn't do it!"

He ignored her. Which didn't sit well with the woman.

"You're a fucking idiot!" she finally exploded. "A fat goddamn fucking moron who shouldn't even be in law enforcement!"

Walter gave her a laugh and a thumbs up.

Chief Goody slowly turned to her.

He'd had just about enough from this white trash slut who thought she was above the law because she was a big shot cable TV personality. If anything, he knew well-enough that her entire family, those deranged bottom-dwelling *animals* living out in the swamp, needed to be locked up.

"Listen to me," he said, dangerously close to just losing it and slapping her across the mouth. "If I hear another word..."

And, still moving, he began lecturing Wendy on the serious consequences of verbally assaulting the chief of police of this fine city, slowly growing even more angry than the woman herself.

He wanted to just *kill* her.

At the same time, Jim Starke did what he did best; he relaxed into a zone of utter blank-mindedness and concentration that usually preceded the untimely death of an unsuspecting enemy of the people.

Wherever.

A tiny lock-pick appeared in his hands, behind his back, dropping down from its always-present place in the sleeve of his sport coat. He silently unlocked Officer Ray's black alloy handcuffs from one wrist, then just as silently dropped the lock-pick to the ground.

A fluid motion later, a small black Para-Ordnance .45 semi-automatic pistol dropped into his right hand from the same sports coat sleeve.

As Officer Ray opened the rear passenger door of the police chief's squad car to accommodate both Jim and Thurman Jr. in the back seat, the Chief himself turned with maximum annoyance from Wendy and leaned forward as he reached for the front passenger door.

Jim simply stepped between Officer Ray and Chief Orville Goody.

He raised the small .45 Para-Ordnance to Chief Goody's head, in the same move lifted his H&K .45 out of Ray Lanyard's hand and pressed that gun into Officer Ray's ear.

Just because he knew the startling effect it always had, he said to both men, "Try not to breathe..."

Officer Billy Jordan saw what was happening and, shocked, started to swing the M16 around but stopped abruptly when he realized he wouldn't live through the follow-up. Not with Jim Starke on the loose.

Officer Ledbetter stood frozen in place, his shotgun pointing straight down.

Thurman Jr. laughed and had to ask, "Holy Christ, Jim-boy, how many guns are you carrying...?!"

Jim pressed the H&K .45 more tightly into Officer Ray's ear, "He stopped looking after the first two."

Which got Ray Lanyard a particularly murderous sideways look from Chief Orville Goody.

Thurman Jr. calmly motioned to Officer Jordan, who rested his M16 against the Chief's car and then unlocked the man's handcuffs. Thurman Jr. put both the handcuffs and the key into his pocket.

Officer Ledbetter had already put down his shotgun.

Thurman Jr. then took both men's handguns, dropped them into his coat pockets, picked up the M16 and the shotgun and then threw them away, far out into the tall sawgrass that surrounded the parking lot.

* * *

Watching with everyone else from a short distance, Sherman Anderson quickly took out his cell phone and called 9-1-1 for assistance.

Pam Jamison saw what he was doing and grabbed at his arm.

"Sherman, don't..." she started.

But the huge man merely swatted her away and listened to the ringing at the other end. If nothing else, he was thinking, Jim Starke and Thurman Jr. might get themselves shot and/or killed with this bold get-away of theirs.

That'd be better than having both of them just rot in jail and, eventually, in prison for years, awaiting certain execution for the murder of Police Officer John Pasco.

Much better.

"Damn it, Sherman—" Pam tried again.

"Shut up." And then, into the phone, "This is an emergency..."

* * *

With Jim still holding Interception City's two top police officers in place, Thurman Jr. moved to Officer Ray and took Jim's Glock 17 and Officer Ray's own custom-made black Colt .45 from him.

Then he found and took Jim's switchblade from the skinny man's pocket.

He said to the officers, "You'll get your weapons back when you boys learn how to handle them. Anyway, stay calm and you'll be okay." He turned to Chief Goody, "It's only about this son of a bitch."

With Jim still statue-still, Thurman Jr. then took Chief Goody's Dan Wesson .357 Magnum from him and pressed the end of the heavy barrel into the Chief's eye at the bridge of his nose.

He thumbed back the hammer.

With two guns pressed tightly to his head, Orville Goody took a steadying breath but suddenly couldn't stop trembling.

Jim told him, "Chief, we need to talk..."

But Orville Goody's anger, especially with half of I.C. standing nearby watching, far outweighed his fear.

He said, "I will see you in Hell before I talk to trash like you. Fuck you!"

Jim nodded, took only a second to decide.

"Hell it is, Chief—"

But the sudden sound of Walter Hightower's .44 Magnum (the hammer unmistakably ratcheting back) caused Jim and Thurman Jr. both to look to Walter—who was aiming the big gun at Jim.

"Guys, this is a real bad move on your part," he told them soberly. "I just can't let you do it..."

Thurman Jr. raised Officer Ray's custom black Colt .45 with his other hand and aimed it at Walter. It was very much a 3-way Mexican stand-off, right out of an old Clint Eastwood movie.

Jim had to smile at the thought.

"Officer Hightower, I appreciate your position," he told the man. "But tell me this: do you believe we'll kill both of these men unless you lower your weapon before I count to one?"

Walter thought it over but then could only nod.

"Yes, I do."

More than anyone standing there, the FDLE officer knew exactly what both men were capable of.

"Oh, God..." Ray Lanyard whimpered.

Jim exhaled, said:

"One—"

And Walter lowered his weapon. Which caused Thurman Jr. to lower the black Colt .45 he held. Neither he nor Walter said a word, just warily watched each other.

Officer Ray Lanyard sagged with visible relief.

Suddenly, in the distance, they could all hear sirens approaching, the other I.C. police cars heading back in a big hurry.

"Jim..." Wendy said. "Now what...?"

He told her, "Stay here with Officer Hightower. You'll be safe with him." He gave the gun he held against the Chief's head a rough push. "Orville, we'll be seeing you again ...real soon."

He and Thurman Jr. started walking quickly towards the back of the huge parking lot.

The two police cars came tearing back, sirens and tires screaming. They screeched to a stop beside Chief Goody and a still badly shaken Ray.

"They're heading for the swamp," the Chief told the returning policemen. "Get an APB out immediately, countywide, escaped cop killers, heavily armed and extremely dangerous."

"It'll be shoot to kill," Officer Ray threw in. Then realized, "Bastards got my custom black Colt..."

Chapter 65

As the two police squad cars that had just arrived took off again through the vehicle-filled lot towards the back. and the jungle behind it, Walter casually moved Wendy aside.

Out of earshot.

"Tell me where the old Bartow place is," he told her.

She gave him a look.

"Do you think they'd have shot you?" she had to know. "Jim or Thurman, I mean?"

Walter gave her a look back.

"Hell, no," he said. "We were just covering my ass. I'm a cop, remember?"

Wendy nodded. Then smiled.

"Good to know."

"Now where's this damn Bartow place...?"

* * *

At the very rear of the large entirely-filled parking lot, Jim and Thurman Jr. saw the I.C. police cars making their way towards them, but at the same time noticed Leonard's black Lincoln sitting alone, engine quietly running.

They shared a look.

"It's eight o'clock," Jim realized. "Guess who that is...?"

* * *

Wendy and Walter, walking back towards the section of jungle Jim and Thurman Jr. had quickly disappeared into, suddenly heard the unmistakable sound of a loud car alarm. It was a car alarm Wendy recognized immediately because it belonged to a Lincoln exactly like her own.

She looked to the sound, in the distance saw the black Lincoln, lights flashing, the alarm going nonstop.

She gestured toward it for Walter's benefit. "Leonard...?"

The both headed back toward it, Walter again drawing his big gun.

A moment later, the two police cars chasing Jim and Thurman Jr. drove past them, then stopped just ahead at Leonard's black Lincoln when they reached it.

Wendy got there next and looked into the vehicle, saw Leonard in the driver's seat, handcuffed to the steering wheel and trying to pull his hand free.

He looked to her, startled to see Wendy outside his car window, but said nothing, just began trying to pull his hand loose even more fervently. In the passenger seat, Wendy saw the judge's briefcase overturned, thousands of dollars in $50 and $100 bills scattered all over the front seat compartment.

She could only stare.

But Walter, far more accustomed in these matters, pulled the driver's car door open and pushed his big .44 into Leonard's startled face.

"Don't move, dirtbag!" the FDLE man said, the second time that day Wendy's husband had had a gun pulled on him. "You're not going anywhere, so stop yanking on that handcuff. Freeze right there, fucker."

And freeze Leonard did, although he wet himself yet again.

* * *

Near the I.C. High School gym, Delmar Spinks walked up to Chief Goody and Officer Ray, both of them standing by the Chief's squad car.

"I told 'em like you said, the old Bartow place," Delmar informed them. He looked like he was about to be sick right there. "But I ain't got the stomach for it no more. I just wanna go back home."

Chief Goody fixed him with a look that held the man in place.

"You're in this until it's finished. Get out there with the boys. We'll get Anderson, be there straight away..."

"It'll be over soon enough," Officer Ray told the skinny man. And then, realizing, he turned back to his father-in-law. "What about Walter Hightower?"

The Chief merely shook his head, wasn't overly concerned.

"First things first," was all he said.

* * *

Heading through a part of the jungle they knew as well as their own backyards, Jim and Thurman Jr. followed a swampy tramped-down dirt path that was well-lit by the very bright moon overhead.

Thurman Jr. took out Jim's switchblade and handed it back to him.

"Here's your knife," Thurman Jr. started. "Anyway, about Wendy..."

Jim could only shrug as they walked along.

"Be pretty hard to resist her," he admitted to his friend. "Even if you did think that love is fucked."

Thurman Jr. nodded.

"Yeah, well—I don't know *what* I was thinking," he said. Then, thoughtfully, "Seems like a nice enough kid, though. That Jennifer. A little ornery but smart."

Jim had to shake his head at the thought.

"Jesus, Thurman, you as a dad..."

"Pretty frightening thought."

"Different, all right," Jim said. "But I guess you never know how it might work out till you try."

"Apparently."

* * *

Wendy and Walter stood by as Officer Billy Jordan, under the FDLE officer's direction, unlocked Federal Judge Leonard Johnson's handcuff from the Lincoln's steering wheel.

Billy pulled Leonard out of the driver's seat, stood him up and re-handcuffed his hands together behind him. He then looked to Walter. The judge was very much on the verge of tears.

"Wendy, I swear..." he tried to start, but then began to actually cry. "Oh, damn, this is so unbelievable..."

"Leonard, you're scum," Wendy told him. "I feel sorry for you, but you're going to be prosecuted for everything you've done—"

Walter said to Billy Jordan, "Officer, formally arrest this man, read him his rights, and gather that money. If he gets out of a cell, or any of that money ends up missing, you'll be arrested, too."

Billy Jordan nodded.

"Yes, sir, I understand."

"Excellent."

Wendy looked to her tear-stained, handcuffed weasel of a husband. Soon to be her ex-weasel-of-a-husband.

"Leonard, you're going to hate prison."

And his tears started all over again.

Chapter 66

Downtown I.C. was pretty much as deserted as it ever was, meaning only a car or two was in evidence at that time of the evening. Thurman Jr. had earlier called in one of the two part-time clerks to run his convenience store, and he was pleased that it all seemed under control.

Through the plate glass window, he could see the young man reading a comic book behind the counter in a store devoid of customers.

Good enough.

Jim and Thurman Jr. crossed the vacant field they'd come out of the jungle into, then moved to Jim's red CJ-5 Jeep, still parked at the I.C. Police department. There were no police cars or police officers anywhere in sight, the building itself lit but locked.

"They're all out looking for you and me," Thurman Jr. said.

"Lucky us."

They jumped into the Jeep and Jim quickly started it.

Several minutes later, they were driving down a narrow jungle trail, lights off, Jim using only the moonlight to guide him.

"Try not to run over a 'gator in the dark," Thurman Jr. advised. "It really pisses 'em off. Then we'll have a whole 'nother fight on our hands."

"Got it."

Jim pulled the vehicle into a hidden clearing not too far from the old Bartow place and killed the engine. They both hopped out, neither one bothering to take off their sport coats.

Jim opened the tailgate, then used a brass key to open a low welded-on metal box in the bed. He reached in, pulled out and handed Thurman Jr. a pistol-grip 10 gauge Ithaca Roadblocker shotgun with a shortened barrel.

He also tossed him a box of Federal shells.

He asked, "You believe Delmar?"

Thurman Jr. shook his head, began loading the semi-auto weapon, putting a few extra shells into his coat pockets

"Fuck, no, that lying cock," he said. "It's a set-up."

Jim exhaled.

"Yet here we are..."

It only took them about ten minutes to get close enough to the falling down shack, the old Bartow place, to spot the small campfire ahead, glowing in the dark. They both dropped down, checked it out from a distance through the thick underbrush.

"Oliver's new home away from home," Jim said. "Impressive."

"I knew old man Bartow," Jim told him. "When he had his still. He'd sit on that porch with a riot gun across his lap, hope the ATF boys'd come out here and start something, just for fun."

"Crazy old bastard."

"That he was," Jim agreed, nodding at the thought. "Thank God we're sane—walking into a set-up like this."

Thurman Jr. gave him a look in the near-dark.

"It's the only way to put 'em all together, sort 'em out after..."

"Right. Spot anybody yet?"

Thurman Jr. gestured. "Oliver's mean ol' boy, Lukas, back by that mangrove clump with a shotgun. He's wearing that stupid hat of his."

They heard a sudden noise, watched as Police Chief Goody's car, lights off, crept slowly up one of the overgrown trails leading to the shack. It stopped well back from the place.

The doors opened quietly.

Jim saw a hand quickly cover the dome light a brief moment, then heard the car doors being quietly closed.

"Three of 'em," Thurman Jr. said. "Looks like we're outnumbered."

Even in the near-dark, Jim could see his friend smile at the thought. He then heard multiple shotguns being racked near the police car, all of it going as slowly and quietly as possible.

"More shotguns," Thurman Jr. said. "Popular weapon."

Jim told him quietly, "If we want to spot 'em all, we better do what they expect—mostly."

With his H&K .45 in one hand and the .45 Para-Ordnance in the other, he suddenly fired both guns into the mangrove clump where he knew Lukas was hiding, got a sharp scream of pain in return.

At the same time, Thurman Jr. used the Ithaca 10 gauge shotgun to blow out half the windshield of Chief Goody's police car.

Not surprisingly, the entire jungle suddenly lit up with flashes of gunfire, all the boys out there hiding and waiting for Jim and Thurman Jr. going wild in an instant. That they'd all panicked at the first shots fired, shots fired *at* them instead of the expected other way around, was obvious.

"Now it's a party," Jim said.

He and Thurman Jr. burst out of the surrounding jungle and zig-zagged to the decrepit shack, bullets and shotgun rounds flying everywhere. Oliver Goody's full-auto AK-47 began firing, tearing up everything it swept across

They reached the front porch, weren't all that surprised when Big Jeff suddenly appeared in the open doorway with his own pistol-grip shotgun. The man fired and hit Thurman Jr. in the side even as Thurman Jr. dove to the right and blasted Big Jeff clear off his feet.

"Christ—" Thurman Jr. cursed.

He'd landed on the porch, hard, but managed to keep hold of the Ithaca, got half-way up to his feet when he was hit again, by one of the other wildly-shooting ambushers, in the legs.

Jim grabbed the back of his friend's coat, dragged him the rest of the way into the shack without bothering to close the bullet-riddled door. The shooting from outside went on, tearing the place to pieces around them.

"Those boys are dead serious," Thurman Jr. said, looked to his bloody wounds under his coat. It was bad. "Son of a bitch..."

"Yeah."

They both looked to Big Jeff, lying on his back on the wooden floor, breathing raggedly, his blood everywhere. As they watched, the man who owned the Alligator Pit gasped once, then stopped breathing.

Chapter 67

Police Chief Orville Goody led Officer Ray and Sherman Anderson, all three carrying shotguns, through the swamp and jungle.

The shooting had stopped, at least temporarily.

They found Oliver Goody with his AK-47, Danny from the junkyard with a deer rifle, Delmar Spinks with his old Springfield but about to throw up, and Oliver's son, Lukas, mostly all bloody.

Oliver couldn't believe it.

"They shot my boy," he said, looking to his brother. "They shot him."

Lukas croaked, "Daddy, I don't want to die..."

"Let's finish this," the Chief said. "It's the only way. Delmar and Danny, get around back."

Delmar looked away, seemed nearer than ever to simply heaving his guts, but he swallowed hard and without a word followed the younger man, Danny, around to the rear of the old shack.

Only a few minutes later, they all opened fired on the place again, riddling it with gunfire from shotguns, rifles and the AK-47.

Inside, as the gunfire destroyed the living room and Big Jeff's body, Jim and Thurman Jr. listened from the kitchen at the rear. They were sitting with their backs against the side of a huge and ancient International Harvester refrigerator that faced the westside of the shack.

"Not very patient, are they?" Thurman Jr. observed.

"Patience is a virtue..."

"I thought patience was its own reward...?"

Jim gave him a look.

"That's virtue."

"They're both virtue...?"

Jim noticed a rifle barrel slide in over the broken kitchen window sill, waited until Danny's face appeared cautiously above it, then shot the young man three quick times with the H&K .45, knocking him back.

Jim said to Thurman Jr., "Let's push."

With their backs against it, Jim and Thurman Jr. managed to push the giant old refrigerator aside several feet. It was more than a minor effort, Thurman Jr. quickly out of breath.

He took a couple of deep breaths to steady himself.

"What the hell'd old man Bartow keep in this thing?" he wanted to know. "Fucking anvils...?"

Jim laughed.

"He had the bottom filled with lead so no one would ever bother moving it," he said, looking at the floor. "There *was* a trapdoor and a tunnel—"

But even in the moonlight, they could both see the wooden floor was smooth, no trapdoor at all to be seen.

"Or not."

* * *

Chief Goody, Officer Ray and the others were spaced entirely around the bullet-riddled shack, effectively blocking any chance of escape. They continued to shoot wildly into the place, hoping to hit *anything* in there.

"They're not shooting back," Chief Goody called out.

He heard Officer Ray call back:

"Let's torch it, let 'em burn—"

Which sounded like a damn fine idea to the Chief.

* * *

As nearly non-stop gunfire continued to tear up the old shack, Jim put his face down close to the floor and blew on the space where the heavy old refrigerator had stood. A fine line suddenly appeared as the dust was blown away.

The trapdoor.

As Thurman Jr. watched, both of them still partly shielded by the old International Harvester refrigerator, and no real gunfire coming from the rear, Jim flicked open his switchblade and worked it into the dusty grove.

With an effort, he levered up the trapdoor and then got his fingers under it.

He lifted it, peered into total darkness.

"Got anything against Black Widow's?" he asked.

Thurman Jr., who he worried was getting weaker by the moment due to blood loss, didn't answer.

"Or poisonous coral snakes?" he tried.

"Love 'em—" his friend finally managed.

* * *

Outside in the surrounding jungle, as the gunfire died down, Chief Goody stepped cautiously into view.

"We mighta got 'em, mighta not..."

He motioned for Officer Ray and Sherman Anderson to do the same. Oliver Goody stepped out, then raked the shack with his AK-47 for good measure. One of the two sons of bitches cornered in there had shot his boy and he wanted them both dead, no matter what.

There'd be no surrendering, no quarter given.

He tipped up the big gun, barrel smoking, and called out to Jim and Thurman Jr. inside, "You boys are alive, give us a yell, we'll work something out..."

When he got no response, he then called over to his son, who hadn't appeared with the others:

"Lukas! You okay, boy? Lukas?!"

Oliver gave his brother Orville a worried look, then moved in the direction Lukas had been shooting from.

He had a very unsettling feeling in the pit of his large stomach that it wouldn't be good.

And he was right.

Chapter 68

Young Lukas Goody sat hidden in the thick foliage he'd been firing from, bloody and hurting throughout it all, head resting back against a wide palm tree. His shotgun was still at the ready, gun smoke still in the air from his last rounds fired at the old shack.

His eyes stared up at the night sky, open wide but now sightless.

* * *

At the old Bartow place, Chief Goody gave a nod and Officer Ray lit a makeshift torch of dry underbrush, gave it a few moments to begin burning brightly, then tossed it through the glassless front window.

They stood watching as the shack began going up in flames.

Behind them, well-hidden but with a clear enough view of the men trying to kill him and Thurman Jr., Jim watched silently.

Half-sitting in the jungle underbrush twenty yards away, Thurman Jr. leaned against a tree breathing weakly. With the 10 gauge Ithaca shotgun lying across his lap, he was almost bled out; the vague thought of simply going to sleep right where he was seemed a pleasant-enough choice for him.

But he was yanked back to reality a moment later when Oliver Goody suddenly poked through the brush trying to find his son, then stopped dead in great surprise when he found Thurman Jr. instead.

"Over here!" the heavy man yelped for his brother. "I got one!"

And Oliver swung his AK-47 around but Thurman Jr. blasted his legs out from under him with the Ithaca, then discovered he was too weak to raise the pistol-grip shotgun again.

He couldn't believe it! His arms and hands were suddenly dead weight with the gun in them.

He could hear Chief Orville Goody, Officer Ray and Sherman Anderson crashing through the underbrush towards him, but could only watch helplessly as Oliver Goody struggled to his knees.

The fat junkyard owner ignored the bloody holes in his pants, managed to lean over and retrieve his fallen AK-47.

"You hurt my boy," Oliver breathed, as his fingers closed around the stock of the big assault weapon. He smiled as he pulled the AK-47 to him, straightened and managed to lift it so it was point blank at Thurman Jr.'s head.

"You ain't so tough now—"

Thurman Jr. had a moment earlier let go of the Ithaca and slid his hand into his coat pocket for the custom black Colt .45 he'd taken from Ray Lanyard, but he knew it was already too late to save himself.

His hand managed to just close around the semi-automatic pistol as he watched Oliver's fat finger tighten, whitening, on the AK-47's trigger, but the quick shot that rang out knocked Oliver over as it took a large portion of the man's head with it.

That single shot had killed the junkyard owner instantly.

Walter Hightower stepped out of the jungle with his big .44 Magnum, looked down to Thurman Jr. with a dark smile.

"Who'd believe I'd be saving your damn cracker ass?" he asked. "It surprises me, too..."

Which was when Chief Goody, Officer Ray Lanyard and Sherman Anderson suddenly filled the clearing, all with shotguns leveled, as they got the drop on both men.

Walter Hightower froze in place.

Officer Ray said to him, "You black son of a bitch..."

But Chief Orville Goody was staring at his brother's lifeless form, the AK-47 next to his body on the ground, couldn't bring himself to believe it.

"Oliver...!"

With almost his last breath, Thurman Jr. slipped the custom black Colt .45 out of his sports coat pocket and shot I.C. Police Officer Ray Lanyard twice in the chest with his own gun.

Chief Goody and Sherman Anderson instantly swung their shotguns around and down to Thurman Jr. lying there, but Jim Starke suddenly appeared from the other side of the small clearing.

With both .45's, he shot them many times just as Walter fired on them as well, the deadly cross-fire cutting both big men to pieces.

As the smoke cleared, Jim and Walter looked around.

Through the dense jungle vegetation the old Bartow shack was still being consumed by flames, at their feet Chief Orville Goody, Officer Ray, Oliver Goody and Sherman Anderson lying dead.

Thurman Jr. half-sat in front of them as well, propped against the tree, breathing faintly but clearly on his last gasp.

"It's the fucking O.K. Corral—" Walter pointed out.

Jim had a sudden thought, called out, "Delmar!"

And heard the skinny man answer from the nearby brush, "They said they'd kill me..."

"What are you doing?" Jim wanted to know.

He heard the man rustling through the foliage, saw him appear with a sheepish look. "I got the diarrhea pretty bad," he admitted. "I didn't shoot none. I saw you come out the tunnel."

Jim nodded soberly.

"Go home, Delmar."

He then moved quickly to Thurman Jr., knelt down. It was obvious his friend was dying, fading too fast to help in any way.

"Thurman,,,!"

The big man didn't respond, had finally lapsed into unconsciousness. In the meantime, Walter was going through Chief Goody's pockets.

"The Chief's car is close," he told Jim. "If we get his keys, get your boy to a hospital—" And then stopped. He said, "Damn."

Walter stood, clearly shaken.

He held up his brother Elmore's gold tooth.

Jim stared at the tooth, looked to Chief Goody's lifeless body with a rising anger that made him clench his teeth. He then heard a soft moaning that caused him to look over to the fallen Ray Lanyard.

He quickly moved to Officer Ray, who was flat on his back, in clear shock, although still alive.

Barely.

The man looked up to Jim Starke with sheer terror in his eyes.

"I've got the keys," Walter suddenly announced.

Jim said, "Walter, if you'll bring the car in quick, I'll have a heart-to-heart with Officer Ray Lanyard here...and find out what really happened."

The FDLE officer gave him a look, then looked to Officer Ray—who looked back to Walter with pleading in his eyes—but Walter shook his head, nodded understanding to Jim, and quickly headed for Chief Goody's car.

Officer Ray's eyes widened as Jim Starke knelt down beside him.

Chapter 69

3 Days Later

In downtown Interception City, it was another perfect day in deep southern Florida, a typically cloudless day of clear blue skies, warm breezes, cocoanut palm trees and 82 degrees in the shade.

Jim Starke, Wendy Jamison and Mr. Thurman Sr. all sat outside on the porch of the huge old Thurman home, Walter Hightower standing before them.

They were all four drinking sweet iced tea.

"So Ray Lanyard's teenage wife was the 'hot-assed little slut' who met your older brother?" Wendy wanted to clarify. "On the Internet?"

Walter sadly nodded.

"That was her."

Jim said, "Virginia Lanyard was Chief Goody's daughter, for some reason married to that idiot Ray. When they found her handcuffed to her own bed with a black eye, I heard she was pretty relieved her husband was dead..."

"I'll bet," Wendy said.

Walter looked to each of them.

"At least we know what happened," he said. "Even though no one's left alive to prosecute. They were lucky, though – corrupt lawmen don't do too well in the joint. I don't think they'd have lasted six months... "

Jim said to Mr. Thurman Sr., "And poor Edna June had nothing to do with any of it. She was just in the wrong place at the wrong time."

A fact which would haunt Jim Starke for the rest of his life, he knew. She'd have never been on that back road if it hadn't been for him. Or for their years-long, highly inappropriate relationship.

Mr. Thurman nodded sadly, but was glad to finally know the truth about her death. At least enough of it to get a measure of closure.

They all jumped when the screen door was suddenly thrown wide open from within with a loud bang.

Thurman Jr. hobbled out, heavily bandaged, on one crutch, young Jennifer under his other arm, helping him.

"I guess I've gained a temporary walking stick," Thurman Jr. said, meaning the girl.

Jennifer gave him a look.

"Try not to be funny—Dad."

The big man looked to her. "I thought you were supposed to be so afraid of me? That's what I heard..."

Which got Jim a sudden glare from the teen.

"Did you tell him that?" she wanted to know. "My dad?"

"It might have slipped out," he told her. "Sorry."

Walter finished his sweet tea, set the plastic glass on the glass-topped patio table, then gave Jim a long look. With a sigh, he took a moment to get out an official FDLE card and then handed it to him.

"Starke, you're a man with some rare skills," he admitted. "Very rare. My Lieutenant wanted me to give you that."

Jim studied the card.

"What, me as a cop...?"

"Probably more like a consultant, a contractor," Walter said. "On an as-needed basis, I'd guess. I'd be putting in a good word for you, of course, as one dangerous badass son of a bitch recommending another..."

Jim had to smile.

"Why, that's very decent of you, Walter."

"Yeah, real white of me," he nodded. "Anyway, "I'm heading back up to Orlando, got a ton of paperwork on this one."

He moved forward, shook hands all around.

"I can't say it was a pleasure, but I do appreciate it. All of it. I never knew any, uh, 'down home' folks as friends."

Thurman Jr. had to laugh.

"Well, you got some now, Walter," he said, finger-shooting him. "We'll expect you at the next hoedown."

"Funny," Walter said as he headed down the porch stairs. "Real funny."

But young Jennifer just rolled her eyes. Grown-ups.

Jim and Wendy walked slowly down the driveway as Walter got into his unmarked car and drove away. They were both careful not to get too close to one another, both careful not to even touch.

They had arrived at what definitely seemed an awkward situation.

"So...what are you going to do now?" Wendy finally asked, not really looking directly at him.

"I'm not sure," he said. He took a breath, tried out what he'd been thinking about the last couple of days, but especially now that he'd been surprised by getting that FDLE card from Walter Hightower: "Orlando *might* be fun, for a change. I was wondering what it'd be like to have an actual life."

He stopped at the end of the driveway, looked to her.

"Maybe you and I could start over," he continued. "Pretend we just met, never knew each other. Go from there—"

Wendy studied him for a long moment, but then shook her head.

"I don't think so, Jim," she said. "That wouldn't work for me. Not a bit."

He nodded slowly. Pretended to understand.

"Right."

"I care way too much about you to pretend I never knew you," Wendy admitted. She looked deeply into his eyes, the electric blue of her own eyes sending a shock wave through him to the core. "Maybe we could try that kiss thing again, see where *that* goes..."

Jim just stared at her. Then:

"That could work."

So he pulled her close and kissed her.

And, after all those years, that was all it really took.

Epilogue

Slightly more than six hundred miles north of Interception City, Jason Kimble sat thoughtfully at his desk at the Palomar Map Company in Atlanta. He was studying the Florida map that Palomar was to publish the following year.

Although young, only 22-years-old in fact, Jason was a computer wizard at the small private company owned by his uncle. He was also solely responsible for checking each city's name for accuracy, for each of the 50 state maps they yearly manufactured.

He'd worked himself into that particular position on purpose, a dreadfully dull assignment, municipality name checking, a position that most of the other employees were not remotely interested in.

"Hmmm," he mused, wondering to himself what name, next year, he would assign to Interception City. He found himself murmuring, "Wanda, Wanda, *Wanda*..."

Originally from Peach Grove, Georgia, he'd long had a secret crush on the teen girl named

Wanda, now Wanda *Elliott*, that he'd gone to high school with, although he'd been a couple of grades ahead of her.

That the 78-year-old mayor of Interception City, that *bastard* George Elliott, had somehow managed to marry the young girl and whisk her away to that hellhole in the Everglades, of all places, irked Jason no end.

Jason did, however, greatly enjoy the old man's heated letters that arrived every year. In fact, he sometimes laughed himself sick at the near-insane anger he was engendering in the old reprobate. Maybe the old bastard would have a stroke if Jason could keep it up for another couple of years, possibly putting a still-young Wanda back on the open market.

It was a thought that caused Jason to smile.

Of course, not a single other employee at Palomar had ever even seen the mayor's livid letters. Or ever caught the yearly error.

Jason thrummed his fingers on the desk for many moments, considering and then discarding many names, before finally smiling to himself and typing into the computer:

Interruption City.

42887481R00181

Made in the USA
Middletown, DE
19 April 2019